CW00516003

SCREENS AGAINST THE SKY

Screens Against the Sky

ELLEKE BOEHMER

BLOOMSBURY

First published 1990
Copyright © 1990 by Elleke Boehmer

The moral right of the author has been asserted

Bloomsbury Publishing Ltd, 2 Soho Square, London W1V 5DE

A CIP catalogue record for this book
is available from the British Library

ISBN 0 7475 0674 4

10 9 8 7 6 5 4 3 2 1

Photoset by Rowland Phototypesetting Ltd,
Bury St Edmunds, Suffolk
Printed and bound in Great Britain by
Butler and Tanner Ltd, Frome and London

'. . . life at that time – in its confinement, its littleness, its negligible engagement with external matters – showed up, precisely by virtue of exclusion, how very much was left out: the entire history of a long struggle, the endurance of that struggle, its effort and its pain.'

It is the late seventies. The townships are burning: a people claims identity, pride, a nation. Meanwhile, two women live in sedentary unease. They are mother and daughter. Locked in adolescent self-absorption, high on diet pills, Annemarie is trying to teach herself politics. Her mother Sylvie is learning to be a widow. She is afraid of hailstorms and the empty sky, and seeks comfort from sweet food, fatherly men, and her daughter's continuing presence.

They both work hard at ignoring the absurdity of their lives, denying, with each glimpse, the uncomfortable realities of the outside world. It is only when Annemarie starts work at a clinic for blacks that the suffocating insularity at home is seriously threatened. In the face of rising domestic tension, her mother goes on cooking, and shopping, collects pretty ornaments and befriends her neighbour, the debonair Étienne Roux. Étienne knows about good food and music; he also knows about Annemarie's friends at the clinic. As events unfold, the relationship between Annemarie and Sylvie is pushed to its limits.

This is a story about South Africa, but indirectly so. That is the point. And the outrage.

CP and MRA

(I am again falling into the wrong tone – and yet I hate
that tone, and yet we all lived inside it for months and
years, and it did us all, I am sure, a great deal of damage.
It was self-punishing, a locking of feeling, an inability
or a refusal to fit conflicting things together to make a
whole; so that one can live inside it, no matter how terrible.
The refusal one can neither change nor destroy; the
refusal means ultimately either death or
impoverishment of the individual.)
Doris Lessing, *The Golden Notebook*

Biko: . . . the black man is subjected to two forces in this
country. He is first of all oppressed by an external
world through institutionalised machinery and through
laws that restrict him from doing certain things, through
heavy work conditions, through poor pay, through
difficult living conditions, through poor education. These
are all external to him. Secondly, and this we regard as
the most important, the black man in himself has
developed a certain state of alienation, he rejects himself
precisely because he attaches the meaning white to all
that is good, in other words he equates good with white.
This arises out of his living and it arises out of his
development from childhood. When you go to school, for
instance, your school is not the same as the white school,
and the conclusion you reach is that the education you
get there cannot be the same as what the white kids get at
school . . . this is part of the roots of self-negation which
our kids get even as they grow up. The homes are
different, the streets are different, the lighting is
different, so you tend to begin to feel that there is
something incomplete in your humanity and that
completeness goes with whiteness.
The Trial of Stephen Biko

PART ONE

It is night-time, early evening. The lights of the house lie along a line. On the left is the kitchen. Below the pots of coriander on the windowsill stares the light bulb in a glass calyx shade. There is no one about. The clock in the stove tells the time but emits no sound. On two cooling racks three pale-yellow sponge cakes lie cooling. The curtains of the next window, partly drawn, leave a slice of light on the lawn. The light cuts into a table, massed with books: at the table, a girl in a dark gym tunic is seated, humped over, tongue crammed into cheek, writing. Her hair, which is greasy, stands on end, skewered into rough tufts around her left ear. Her right hand works at speed; she cannot keep her eyes off it. Her left lies flat on the page with the careful, balancing action of a child who first learns to form letters – as though she were pacifying the pace of the words. At moments when she looks up, this hand drifts back to her head, around the ear, there to work and twist.

At the far end of the house lies what must be the living-room. At all angles stand chairs, occupied by trim rotund cushions, lapped in brocade antimacassars. On the sofa, facing the open window, sits a woman. She is reading, though she has also been knitting. She gets up and walks over to the piano. Momentarily, her hand lies spread over the keys. She looks down at the keyboard, but thinks better of it. She walks back to the sofa, picks up the magazine. She fumbles with an attached perfume sample; the sachet will not come open. She sits down. She reaches for the portable radio at her side. Her thumb and forefinger are pursed around the on/off knob, but she thinks better of it. She settles back in the sofa. There is no sound about. The TV is flickering.

It is midnight. There are two lights on in the house. One is on in a bedroom. Two beds stand in close parallel, separated by a bedside table; only one bed is turned down. On the bedside table, painted buff eggshell off-white, lies a New English Bible, abutting on a colonnade of pill phials. On the bed are spread a long nightshirt and pyjama trousers, the elastic slacked into bagginess. There is no one about. The young girl must be asleep because in the other lit window, elongated like a Cranach figure by the effect of framing, the woman is visible. She is standing at the table where the girl was working. As with the girl, the woman's head is bent over the books. The sickle of chin brackets that of nose. She moves her hands in amongst the books, stops herself, moves the books again. She spends some time in this manner, shuffling, pausing, shuffling, then retreats to the bedroom empty-handed. She does not forget to turn off the light.

During my adolescence I kept a journal. Or, to speak more precisely, journal writing occupied most of my early adolescent years. If I had its various volumes with me now, I could give a fuller account of that time. I say fuller, I might say richer, but not more accurate. If accuracy was the law of journals, I did not see that there was any point. No matter how I might press them, my days did not give out a sweetness that seemed worth distilling. I was interested not in the quotidian present, not in the passed past, but in the future, from which point of view everything might be retold. I never spent time so contentedly as when I was reviewing time: undoing and then reforming the done thing. At times I took this process right back to basics. Instead of adjusting story and fact to conform to one another, I styled the facts of my life to fit the story. I might create the mood or say the words that would suit the girl in the journal – an interesting girl, as I saw her, dark-eyed, young, and solitary, and a book-bound recluse. The thing to get right, though, was ambience – a pervasive feeling of quietude; the preparation for insights of premature sagacity and penetration. Mostly, creating this feeling was not too difficult; there weren't too many props I had to worry about. Vacant hours spent staring out of a bedroom window take their muted colour even from a tune played in an adjoining room, or a fly burring against the glass.

One reading venture alone, one that was sustained over weeks, I consciously designed to bring about an entirely new kind of existence, generous but committed, and very stern. I would, I decided, take the affairs of the nation to heart. I tried so hard I began to copy out newspaper reports, to write what I was reading straight into the journal. At the time the effort was almost wholly successful. I felt I was interested or – even more than that – involved. Precisely because of the rigorous reading I was doing, I was able to ignore the fact that I had exempted myself from other activity. The reading made all the action, and was exciting enough.

I begin by saying all this because what follows may in part be drawn from the memory not only of what happened, but of what I once wrote happened. I do not set out to re-create those fictions; but as I have no way now of reviewing them, as I no longer have the journal books in my possession and cannot check up on my memories, I can never be sure that my present account did not in part begin on the pages of my journal. If I spent so much time on the journal, it is possible that details of what I remember of those last school years did not in fact happen – details of Father's death, say, and the retreat to my bedroom; the encounters with Simon, and also what happened immediately thereafter, during that second summer vacation after Father's death. So I will begin by making my account as succinct as possible; it will be a way of cutting out – of writing off, you could say – the fabricated facts.

Of the later years which also have a place in this account, I am not much more certain, though by then I was no longer keeping the journal. By then I had so erased writing and memory exercises from my daily routine, and days were so much the same, that a similar problem appears in a new form. Is what I think happened what I now believe happened? It might well be so.

Having said this, I will admit to having about me a few pieces of hard evidence to touch off my memory; they are not very many, it is true, but are still representative enough: two pages taken from newspapers; a folded flyer in green paper; two homemade dinner menus, one written, one typed on mauve card; and a photograph. The photograph is of my mother, tall and bony, standing in between me, somewhat shorter, and a friend of hers, who is also tall. It was taken one evening with a flash – our eyes glow red. I also hold on to a useful and very simple guiding idea, which is this: that if I spent most of my time in a sort of adolescent stupor, unaware of the actual passing of time, then that – exactly that – was my experience. Day-dreaming and writing and absent-minded gazing was what I was doing, and that is what I must record. Does this seem to be an odd and perhaps distorted picture? Do I betray that I was concerned, almost obsessively concerned, with nothing so much as with my own self? Yet this is, I suppose, my intention. I believe my preoccupation at that time was in itself telling. I believe that my life then – in its confinement, its littleness, its negligible engagement with external matters – shows up, precisely by virtue of exclusion, how very much was left out: the entire history of a long struggle, the endurance of that struggle, its effort and its pain.

The Rudolphs had lived in the town of Merrydale since Annemarie was two, lived quite comfortably though always frugally in a bungalow house called Tintagel. In Merrydale the weather, especially during the summer months, was often unpredictable, and when unpredictable, unkind. Sylvie Rudolph, sweating into her square-cut cotton blouses carefully conserved from the fifties, sat out the heat with her feet immersed in ice baths. In the heat, they longed for the thunderstorms to break, but, when the coolness came, it was with ferocity. Pacing, keeping close to inside walls, Sylvie winced with the lightning and called upon her father. By the end of the storm when the hail covered the lawn and flowerbeds in snowy piles – or, if things turned out unluckily, lay also on the living-room carpet and chairs, scattered in amongst cushions and shards of broken glass – Sylvie would be crouched under the dining-room table, her legs clamped to her chest, and her arms around her legs. Later, when order was restored, she would observe that, as she saw it, Europeans were never meant to endure this climate. 'It's a madness,' she said. 'Barbaric. We should have gone beyond this.'

In her journal her daughter Annemarie might record: 'Another storm. Lots of sheet lightning. Mother again distraught.'

Sylvie's fear had grown fiercer since John's death. John Rudolph died in the dry winter month of June. The first storm of the new rainy season – an ambitiously big display – occurred three and a half months later. It had been afternoon; Annemarie was at school. Sylvie was still on the tranquillisers prescribed by the doctor after John's death.

The storm came up so suddenly, Sylvie did not have time to close the windows. As she fled for the table, she was arrested by a smash of lightning. She paused long enough to see the big casuarina at the end of the garden immolated in a slender plume of fire. Calling, 'Father, Father,' she ran towards the telephone, but the lightning seemed to be snatching at its wires. The instrument pipped and shivered. Sylvie was afraid to go near it.

By the time Annemarie got home, various neighbours had come round to inspect the charred spike of what had been the tree. Geoff from next door, and Tim from up the road, with their hands in their pockets, stood kicking bits of bark and wet wood, by turns shaking their heads at the tree and looking askance at Sylvie. It was the first time that they had come into the yard since John's funeral. With the paternal solicitousness of a man who has his self-esteem in mind, but is loath to incur responsibility, Geoff had at first come to stand close to Sylvie, in order, perhaps, to take her elbow. He impressed upon her his certainty that the municipal people would come round within the week to remove the tree. Sylvie, having taken three Valiums, gazed at him vacantly in response. Now Mrs Roberts, from four doors up, the house with the handsome azalea garden and the swimming pool, had taken responsibility for the elbow and with her free hand supported the tea mug Sylvie was half-heartedly holding.

'Get your boy to clear the mess when he comes on Saturday,' Mrs Roberts soothed. 'He's a good boy. Just promise me not to touch it yourself.'

Sylvie turned the abstracted stare towards her.

'You've had a lot to deal with recently,' Mrs Roberts continued. 'You must take it easy.'

In something of a conversational manner, Sylvie moved to confront her face-on.

'Yes,' she said with emphasis, as though in direct response to her remark. 'Yes, as John always said, that's how it will be if the blacks do come. That's exactly how I imagine it will be. A mass of fire. See what it can do. It is too terrible for words.'

During the weeks after the storm, the hailscreens of pine slats and chicken wire – the ones John Rudolph had constructed to protect the plate-glass expanse of the living-room picture windows – were installed at each west-facing window of the house. Sylvie had Simon make them, following the sketches which John had left tacked up in his toolshed. Originally, they bought the house for the view. From most of the main rooms – the master bedroom, Annemarie's room, the living-room, even from the kitchen – the view led out over broad farmland and veld, smoothing away to the hills. John had enjoyed this view. Especially during his last illness, he had spent his afternoons on the verandah, gazing out over the land. At a time when Annemarie was smaller and younger, he had liked to place her between his knees, take her hand and point it towards the far horizon.

'Look at that beauty,' he would instruct her. 'Drink it in. That – all of that – is our land.'

Sylvie, alone after his death, felt differently about it. The long slope of the veld leading up towards the hills drew her own eyes towards the sky and the bleak white sun. There was too much space about. She preferred not to see it. With the chicken wire netted across the windows, she could focus on something close at hand. The screens made a web to which her skittering eye might cling. It was a protective covering – on fine days, as well as during storms. Annemarie might complain about the ugliness of it: from the outside, Annemarie said, the house looked bleary-eyed; from within, vision was blurred. But to Sylvie that was the point. So satisfied was she with the effect that she had Simon do others, for the back windows also. It was absurd to have only one side of the house protected. You never could tell whether the hail would come from the other side, during a freak storm. It was important to feel safe all round.

In Merrydale in April or September, autumn or spring, it can be warm but it is rarely too warm. It is the time when, in the garden at Tintagel, the soil must be turned. At this time, beneath its dry outer skin, the earth shows moist and soft.

Sylvie had instructed Simon how to mulch: he must stamp on the spade like this, he must go in deep, he must toss the clods right over. He must work hard just as she has shown him and at five he can have his lunch.

The mulching takes up most of the day. Simon bends and straightens, bends and straightens; stamps on the spade, tearing weed, splitting clods; tosses the soil; inserts the spade again. All day he sucks a grain kernel he has found lodged between his teeth, tips it out on to his bottom lip, sucks it back in again. Off and on he hums a tune, letting the sound resonate in his cheek bones. The work is not very interesting. Simon spends time staring down the street, over the split-pole fence, looking out for passers-by. Whenever the sun feels a little lower, he squints up at the house. Lunch-time is long in coming. It's difficult to work out what is happening up there, to see if they are stirring. There seems to be no movement inside the house, no sound. From this distance, due to the hailscreens and the reflections in the glass, the windows are entirely opaque. Simon turns his eyes down the street again.

Next door Simon hears someone knocking planks together. The hammer goes tock, and tock. Several houses away, a lawnmower is whirring. Simon stamps on his spade again; the spade tears the soil. The sounds seem loud because the street is very quiet. Simon watches a dog slope down the length of the hedge opposite. He sees that two mynahs have landed on the table that stands on the verandah up at the house; the birds are checking for crumbs. For hours no one has been about; Simon has not heard another human voice. It almost seems as though the white people in this neighbourhood – the house owners, that is – had left town.

A puzzle I have set myself is to piece out, of those four years recorded and then lost, one or two reference points, to get my bearings; to say, Here I am beginning. I have used the word puzzle, but on second thoughts the exercise is perhaps not really that difficult. It was my habit to intersperse the more dilatory passages in my journal with short declarative notes. These lined the white spaces between the closely written paragraphs and so blocked off the different sections. In a few brief statements, I recorded the event of my father's death, in June 1976. I noted down the date of the family quarrel two and a half years before, the time we went up to Cantonville for Christmas; I also noted the day of the thunderstorm that brought down the casuarina tree. So in a way I have some facts to go by, notched in my memory as sentences.

I will remember the time in Cantonville – it is the earliest date, and makes a clear image, one of the clearest I have of my father. At that time my journal was in its beginning stages – written by fits and starts; it was after his death that I began to use it to fill up time.

The way I remember it, Father broke with his brother after a political squabble that began on Christmas Eve and continued until Boxing Day. Father thought his brother, Felix, was leaning too far left. Felix believed in reform, that is, he wanted rules about separate amenities scrapped. Father believed, he strenuously pronounced the words, in plurality and cultural specificity. To me he did not explain what he meant. He said these things were not yet for me to know. Mother, even after his death, declined to define. She explained she did not know herself – or not precisely – but, knowing Father as she did, thought that he was probably right. But Felix called Father heartless and atheist. Father said he was an atheist and proud of it. He stood in the middle of the living-room at Felix's, each foot planted squarely on a large verdigris bloom in the floral carpet, as though supporting himself on lilypads.

'Sylvie!' he shouted. 'Sylvie!'

She came up running.

'Sylvie,' he said, staring across at Felix, 'get out the car.'

Mother ran hither and thither to find the keys. I sat on the rattan sofa, waiting to see whether it would be Uncle Felix or Father who would break the silence. Neither did. They stood there, unmoving, looking alike: both flushed with anger, both squat.

When we heard the car drive round to the front, Father began to stride towards the door.

'Come,' he said to me.
I followed.

We stayed at the Cantonville Hotel that night. The next morning Mother went back to Felix's for our suitcases. Then we drove home. The sun lay hard on the land. Dust devils flung across the veld. Once the path of a dust devil crossed ours. We were momentarily lost in a swarm of dust-smatterings. Father brooded all the way; Mother knitted, nodding understandingly whenever he broke out to rail against Felix. I sat in the back, sliding on the seat in my own sweat, inspecting my pimples in a hand mirror, and eating I do not remember what out of a tin or a jar – Aunt Elna's apricot jam, perhaps, or condensed milk.

Very clear in my mind is the way Father used to drive, like on the trip back from Cantonville, leaning just slightly forward, hands cramped at the top of the wheel. He had the habit, I remember, of occasionally switching his knee when driving, quite suddenly and with startling force, using the back of his hand. I used to think he was reminding himself of something important, or perhaps showing us that the heat of the sun on his legs was too strong. He didn't tell us, though, Mother and me, what might be troubling him.

In the car when driving – but sometimes in the living-room, if she was sitting in a chair beside him – I also remember Father putting out his hand to touch Mother's leg. He would fit his cupped hand over the ball of her knee. He let it rest there just an instant, then withdrew it, still cupped. I see it like that – the big stubby hand curled in mid air – it is a slight memory; also a silent one. If she was not knitting during car drives, Mother sat tight and said very little and kept her eyes on the road.

*   *   *

After Cantonville, Father's death was the first big event in my journal. There I placed him, right at the beginning of the book, as a kind of headpiece to everything that followed.

Mainly I remember Father in his sick-bed, as I saw him last. Every day he called to me to come and read to him from the newspaper – the first and the third pages. It was essential, he insisted, to keep up to date with international news. As for the rest, home affairs, we could rest assured the government was taking care of that. He said I might put questions to him. I did. What, I might ask, what are these homelands, these separate zones, shaded areas piebald on the map? What is plural representation? But he would reply with a question: Who the hell have you been speaking to? And so our attempts at bedside conversation ended. Then he grew too sick to talk. Then he died. My father died in June 1976. Around the middle of the month. At that time I was not reading the papers.

At that time, I was writing in my journal – there is no way I can mistake this memory, the words were arranged down the page in a column – my father is dying; my father is dying; my father is dying. Put that way the whole thing was easier to believe.

Had he not died, it might not have been a very memorable winter. At school discos everyone was wearing Stars and Stripes T-shirts to commemorate the Big Bicentennial. At school the girls who were 'in' and knew things copied Rod McEwan poems into their scrapbooks and traced out 'Love is . . . ' pictures. They hummed 'Don't Go Breaking My Heart' as they changed for gym. In the local pharmacy, on an errand to get either Father's – or maybe Mother's – pills, I discovered slimming tablets called Slenderettes, white and translucent orange capsules that made you sweat. I discovered that the least stressful mode of existence was to spend time in my bedroom, with the curtains partly closed against the glaring light, sitting quite still and listening to my heart race.

Sometime during the week before he died, my father, struggling with the rasp in his throat, told me to go on being a good girl, to remember who my father was and what he had stood for; not to neglect my mother who was dear to us and not to listen to the fools who, in my gullibility, might waylay me.

I sat at his hospital bed holding his pincer hand with one hand and fiddling with the poinsettia on the side table with the other. I noticed that his water jug was empty and that the doily beneath it was plugged full of dirt. I said yes, Father, yes, of course, yes.

Nothing is quite so traumatic as the death of a spouse. Sylvie Rudolph could vouch for it. The proof is all there; in the tables of relative shock impact in the women's pages of newspapers you see it illustrated. But you have to experience it yourself; then only will you know what it all really means.

Since John's death, in the middle of the year, when the garden lawn was turning brittle underfoot and the sunsets were crimson with dust, things had so changed for Sylvie – even though gradually – that she could not work out quite where she was now. Nor what she should do. She had not at first suspected it – how small and single you would start to feel. The thing was that the change was subtle. The newspapers explained it happened gradually – it was the system's way of adjusting. So you were caught unawares. You thought you were managing, you stopped taking tranquillisers, and then one day you did something quite ordinary – turned a

corner or dropped a tea towel – and then suddenly you saw:
My life is empty and I am lost.

On the surface, as people said it would, existence went on
as usual. There on the wall above the fireplace was the same
picture, the desert landscape, and here, you were sitting on
the same chair. You did not age overnight; Annemarie did
not immediately grow up. Rump steak with green peppers
and chips on Friday nights – always John's special meal –
tasted just the same as before. And the smell of him lingered
– the pipe smoke in the living-room, and against the cushion
he used for napping, the smell of his hair.

A big help of course was that the two of them wanted for
nothing, were exactly as comfortable as before. John – it was
so much his nature – had left them well provided for. The
money was stacked into the stable shares on the stock exchange, where – this was his expression – gold and dia-
monds are for ever. Naturally, you couldn't help worrying
sometimes about the market being so responsive to international pressures when it was clear that the outside world
had no idea at all how to manage the situation in the country.
But still, up to this point, they were living as they always had,
and would, God willing, continue to do so. As a kind of
thanks to John for this, Sylvie carried on with the household
accounting system he had devised, noting down in a narrow-
ruled exercise book, item by item, all that they spent –
including, a little uncomfortably, the carnations, white ones
– for the funeral. It gave a sense of connection with him to
do this. And that is what a person needed – something to do
that reminded you of the past.

So it wasn't a material lack that made things different.
Nor was it his physical presence – him, the body – that you
particularly missed. It was something almost inexpressible,
deeper and closer, against the floor of your mind. This was
why it took longer to manifest itself. Maybe it lay in the feeling

that John was – how straightforward the words were – not there: not there in the house with you, within calling distance and ready to listen. It lay in the knowing that he would not again be around for talk, over coffee in the evening, for example, or when you woke up in the middle of the night, before the dawn, feeling alone. So here the women's pages had it wrong. They said it was the body closeness that mattered. But that wasn't it really. Because you couldn't miss what you hadn't really wanted. Those encounters had never lasted very long, and, anyway, it was difficult to see their point. It was rather the voice you missed, and the company.

Thinking about missing him, Sylvie admitted that for many months, many, many months, before he died, she had tried to avoid John in bed. From the very beginning, afterwards – that is, right from the first days of their marriage, after they'd been together – she had always inched back to her own bed; and in the morning, she was thankful, he was always up before her. It was after the birth of their little one, small Annemarie, their only one, she had started to lose interest. One time they did it after a gap of almost a year. The sweat coming off him, she remembered, had collected in the runnels of her stomach. And his body lying beside her had looked greyer than before, as though coagulated soap suds had settled into the folds of his skin. If she was not sure before, that experience had decided her. But as it turned out, there had been no need to say anything about it. He sickened soon after that: there was his prostate trouble, together with the heart; then the prostate again, the cancer this time, and the long ailing. But even despite this, the many months of disease, his death had still seemed so unexpected. She had not minded nursing him, had grown used to it. And then suddenly he was dead. One day to the next. Her husband.

These kinds of thoughts are difficult to ignore. Sometimes, lying beside his empty bed at night, Sylvie wondered if she had done completely right by John. One kiss more when he asked it of her? Or a soft word when he placed his hand on her knee? When he was ill, she had cared for him; when he was well, she had kept away. You miss, yes, how you miss, his advice, his help, his company in conversation – but not the other, the breathing shape in the dark at night, in that next bed. Not that. For this reason Sylvie did not want another man. Her sisters urged her solicitously in their letters, but she would not think of it. She could not even conceive of it. Some old body, shrunken flanks and buttocks, here in her bed: it was not what she needed at all.

But her main point was that there was no one to touch John. He had taken account of her needs – of everything she wanted, even the lying apart. Naturally, the child dominated her attentions – this is the way of mothers; but, as will happen when you have the right man, it was John who stood at the centre of her existence. You feel your husband's absence precisely because he makes up your life.

John had done everything for Sylvie. It was always John who went shopping in town. He walked the extra blocks to get the bargains she marked in green felt pen on the shopping list; he even walked down to the Indian shops to find the wool and the cloth that was cheapest and best. He was the one who answered the telephone, who made their holiday bookings and checked Annemarie's homework. With bridge parties too he was in charge. He always invited the three other players. Sylvie brought out the drinks and small eats – miniature gherkins and pâté and melba toast; and his favourite bite-sized sausage rolls, and the mayonnaise dip with boiled egg mashed up in it – and then she went to sit in the room next door to the living-room, which was a sort of study. She liked to knit there, and to watch silent TV.

Before her marriage Sylvie had been a church-goer. But that ended soon after meeting John. John had discouraged her from going. Perhaps she had not always been a true believer, at least not at that time, when she was a girl, but Mother and Father had gone, and so their daughters had gone along with them – Elizabeth and Sarah and Sylvia and Christina, four tall sisters with respectable singing voices. Sylvie had liked to go. She liked the cool and grey quiet in a church. She had taught Sunday School for many years, too. But John had put a stop to all of that. Sylvie had been disappointed not to marry in a church. The child often asked where the wedding pictures were. There were ones of Elizabeth and Sarah and even Christina, though that had been an unfortunate affair, lasting less than two years. But she and John had been married on a Tuesday morning, without parents or photographer. He had wanted it so. Thereafter, on Sundays, they had read the papers and fried up a big breakfast and had a small dry sherry before lunch. Sundays, for the last few years, though, had not been that special; John, being retired, was at home all week anyway. But they had spent time together easily, not saying very much, drinking coffees, waiting for Annemarie to come home from school and tell them her news.

For the spouse the loss will always be greater than for the children. Again, the women's pages said it. And yet sometimes – though it did seem an odd thought – Sylvie wondered if Annemarie had not endured the bereavement surprisingly well. It was when he was dying that Sylvie had first started to wonder about her: small Annemarie standing at the window, looking out dry-eyed while her father was dying. Even Simon, the garden boy, had shown a little more compassion. Simon, the boss is dead, she told him at the kitchen door when he returned after that long winter break. Ai, madam, he said, shaking his head and shuffling his feet. Ai, madam. When the nurse came into the waiting-room to tell them John had gone, Annemarie had picked up the exercise book she had been carrying with her for all of those long weeks and had started to write. She had been writing ever since, first in the dining-room, and now more and more often in her bedroom. Sylvie wished she wouldn't. She decided to tell her so before long. It was a big house: if you didn't spend time together, you grew lonely.

Of course she and John had often kept to themselves when they were alone together in the house. But that was different: they knew each other well; they felt no need for words. Sometimes they used not to speak from one meal end to another. Sylvie knew most of his stories off by heart, the ones he told with all that loud bravura at his bridge parties: what he did in the war, what the other fellows were doing in the war, what he did after the war and what he would rather have done. As the years go by, Sylvie had found, you run out of approving responses. In general you find there is less and less to say. After they had discussed Annemarie's progress at school or her future prospects, he did not want to hear about knitting patterns, or how Sylvie's alyssum – recently transplanted by Simon – was growing. When she asked him if he wanted coffee, she never waited for a reply; and she listened in silence to his angry commentary during the news on the radio. In the last years it was mainly the oil crisis and the oil embargo imposed on the country by those who did not know better that upset him. Perhaps he should have taken things a little more calmly. Still, at the time you drew comfort from his faith in the nation. When the world was falling into small pieces around them, he would say, smacking his knee, when all was confusion and empty-headed idealistic nonsense, this country – founded on good sense, and courage and conviction, as they all knew – would stand strong. She believed him.

Because of her loneliness, it was a blessing there remained enough for Sylvie to do in the house and in the garden. You must find ways to fill up the emptiness; that, said everyone – the house doctor, the journalist – was rule number one. John, thank goodness, had always refused to employ a house servant: he said it was a luxury they could do without; he was bringing in enough money for his wife not to have to go out and work. So there was the whole house to look after, and Annemarie to cook and care for. As for the garden, Simon came in only on Saturdays and the place had run to riot during the time of John's illness. John had also insisted that important tasks be completed after his death: the reinforcement of their split-pole fence, and the conversion of the flowerbeds to lawn. So there was lots of straightening and tidying to do.

You also couldn't forget the condolence letters. That is at least a task you feel you can still perform for the departed. Sylvie arranged the letters on John's desk, area by area and province by province, in neat piles. He would be proud of her, the way she found something personal to say to each one of his past colleagues, golf mates, bridge partners, sisters-in-law. To John's estranged brother Felix she sent a particularly long reply. She told him it was pointless to feel guilty about not coming to the funeral. He and John, Sylvie was quite sure, had been united in the end. When all was said and argued out, they shared their love for this fine land and their belief in it.

Sylvie had a few bad days of wandering aimlessly round the house when the condolence replies came to an end. Time moves on, it is true, but its passage seems very slow. You redust the piano, rearrange the ornaments, the Chinese brass vases, a little closer together. The antimacassars must be smoothed so that the weft faces away from the light. But then suddenly you catch yourself standing still in the middle of the room and your hands hanging idle. What do you do? How can you telephone people in this sort of state? Even if you call

Elizabeth, who lives closer than Sarah and Christina and whose voice on the phone is quiet and undemanding? What if you open your mouth and there are no words in it? There seems to be nothing to say. There is no news.

Because she no longer played the piano – John had always been her audience, she couldn't play without him – Sylvie began to sing to herself, usually snatches of Schubert *Lieder*, as she knitted. Singing disguised the peremptory way the needles clicked off the minutes; singing also exercised her voice. What if you lose the confidence to form words, Sylvie sometimes worried, not only on the telephone, but even when you're face to face with people? Perhaps, she thought, the less you speak now, the less you will ever be able to speak. Loneliness is like a social mistake; you get to feel so vulnerable – vulnerable and sore about being so alone and nervous about ever being with people again. That was why Sylvie felt safer after they put in the hailscreens as a permanent fixture. The hailscreens literally filled in the gaps: the gaping holes of windows and the huge loneliness of the sky.

Weekday lunch-times at Tintagel are very slow. At twelve-thirty when morning concert ends on the radio, Sylvie Rudolph puts on a small pot of water to boil. When the water is boiling, she lowers into the pot a medium-sized grade two white egg. While waiting for the egg to cook she goes to unlock the front door that Annemarie locked behind her on her way out to school this morning. Sylvie, too, goes out and locks the door behind her. She has the bunch of house keys with her. She walks round to the verandah, lifts down the hailscreen that protects the glass door leading out from the living-room, dusts the top edge of the screen a little with her apron, then lets herself in. She returns with a plastic plaid-patterned tray bearing left to right a mug of tea, a paper napkin tucked in under the mug, a saltcellar, two teaspoons, one knife, the egg in a cup, a buttered sandwich on a plate and a glass finger-bowl full of after-dinner chocolates. She places one of the verandah chairs so that it faces the house. Here she sits. She eats. She cuts up her sandwich into small cubes. She unpeels each chocolate carefully, and places it in the middle of the plate and looks at it a moment before eating it. Now and then she checks her reflection in the glass door. She pats her hair. She rubs at spots on the table with her used paper napkin. She sits. After some time she puts her tray just inside the door, locks up, hangs the hailscreen again, walks once round the house, slowly, and goes back indoors.

So I have memories, I think more or less accurate, mainly of single memorable events. But, even if I string them together, these events do not seem to create a continuous flow of time. What I want is a way of recalling the commonplace days, the recurring impressions – images of spoons in a rack or the design and variegated colour of the floor parquet – that I missed out when I wrote my journal. I don't have a way of hooking the single discrete happenings on to a wider backcloth of everyday. So I might remember Christmas Day in Canton-ville, but not Mother's hairstyle at the time, or whether Father was already ill. My eyes, no doubt, were riveted on myself. The clothes I wore, the food I ate; these I remember more clearly.

Remembering these things, it helps that my wardrobe most of the time showed very little variety. Until about my fifteenth year, Mother continued to make my clothes on her hand-propelled Singer. Clothes for Mother always meant dresses, cut according to a basic shift pattern. Father and Mother believed in thrift, and the two Indian stores in Merrydale sold off serviceable cottons at equally serviceable prices. As time went on, and I began to swell and thicken at breast and hip, Mother began to make these dresses on a principle of infinite extension; over years a hem could be repeatedly dropped, pleats replotted. I thought of bags of sprouting potatoes and balked. I went on my first diet. For two days I ate only water biscuits – then Mother made one of her caramel fridge cakes. I had not yet discovered appetite suppressants. That came a little later. At the time it was difficult to resist Mother, both in matters of food and of clothes.

Usually Mother would cut out three or four dresses in one afternoon. She would display them on my bed, puffed and smoothed out in the right places. Her persuasive suggestions to leave out the ruches and the smocks, and so accommodate her amateurism and my bosom, had their effect. I agreed to the orange floral, the green floral, the pink prickle-dot, and the plain white. They were dresses my friends stared at in frank interest. The promised looseness of the abandoned ruches did not happen in practice; instead, the plain straight fronts squashed my breasts to pat-a-cake shapes.

Encouraged, it may be, by the capacious and unabashed ugliness of these creations, my new curves plumped into soft fat. I fell asleep at night with one hand pressed against the warm underside of my belly. It was comforting that way. Clearer even than the image of my dresses are my memories of the food Mother and I engulfed. Around the time of my first menstruation it was egg-nog, big mugfuls that would slip down in one glutinous swallow. Egg-nogs turned us on to sloppy rice puddings, and after that homemade ice-cream, creamy fudges, fridge cakes in all sorts of stages of crunchiness and gooeyness, and chocolate puddings. Mother believed in the virtues of a well-lined stomach. A growing girl needs her milk and sugar, she said. She might skimp on bacon, but she slipped chocolates under my pillow. On Saturday mornings we mixed up viscous messes and set them on the middle shelf in the fridge ready for easy access all weekend. Anything that flopped we gave to Simon, who did not say no to such rich and milky treats.

Simon was around regularly in those days, both before the winter of Father's death, and after. His image, for the greater part, blends in with the matte background of things: he filled in Mother's flowerbeds to create more lawn – only to open them up again later; he built most of Mother's hailscreens; after Father's death he took over his big black mug, the one that said 'Our Dad' in gold writing. He must have been around every Saturday, except for the months around Father's death, around June. He became important to me later on, just before he left for good and we moved house. At the time of the early stages of the journal, though, his figure makes an uncertain shape. I did not notice him.

During the months after John's death Sylvie could not stop thinking about emptiness, and the thoughts frightened her. It might seem a strange thing to have in your mind – emptiness – yet there it was, right in the middle of her thoughts, no matter what she did. The way Sylvie saw it, the universe was full of matter – as an egg is, or a fruit – bulbous with its own fullness. There was nothing that did not contain something: a womb was either swollen with blood or with child, a fist was full of fingers and the night of dreams. Nothing could be reduced to nothing: a human life to a few photographs, the memory of a voice and the stale smell of pipe smoke in a cushion, or, sometimes, very faintly, in the binding of favourite books. But what else was there? A few days after John's funeral, the undertaker had called about his ashes. Sylvie told him to hold them for a while. For the moment, there was nothing she could think of to do with them. What were ashes really, what could they signify? All they showed was that John wasn't around any more.

When her own father died, Sylvie and her sisters had scattered his ashes on the open veld, but they had gone home afterwards feeling even more bereft. Their little ceremony was awkward. They had driven out on the Sandvliet road to a designated high knoll, not quite a *koppie*, out of sight of human habitation. This was an advantage because, as Christina pointed out, and they all agreed, you did not want undesirables looking on. They climbed out of his old blue station wagon at the gate by the side of the road, lamely clutching their light summer skirts to their thighs. It had been windy.

The trig beacon to which their father had directed them was some way from the road. They tottered their way over clumps of grass and dense whorls of dandelion. Elizabeth warned them about ticks; Sarah said it was snakes that worried her. At the beacon Elizabeth sang a hymn, 'Nearer My God to Thee', before spilling out the contents of the sturdy plastic bag they had brought with them. Christina joined in with her, but in tremulous snatches. Sarah was looking away and crying. To Sylvie, the hymn sounded not so much timorous as superfluous. The wind washed away the words and blew bits of ash into their faces and against their legs.

Back home, she told John about it. He had scoffed and said of course the whole thing was quite absurd; what did they expect? When his time came, they should dump what was left of him in a bin. It was useless to pretend that anything more glorious was going on in some other place. He for one did not believe it. His lips were pulled in white over his teeth by the vehemence of his utterance. He said, Do not forget my words.

Sylvie had obeyed him. She could not forget these words. That was part of her difficulty. If only he had believed, as her father had, that if you were lucky something might just happen afterwards, even though you could not be quite sure. Then she might feel a little better. But instead it was as though he had wilfully committed himself to oblivion. He had left only hollowness behind him – clothes sagging on their hangers, a double dent in his desk chair, big empty rooms. Surrounded by his discarded things, Sylvie feared that in his case nothing would follow, nothing but hollowness. It was like a kind of vengeance. Because he had wanted it so.

Sylvie decided to call in a minister of the faith when it began to appear that the hours of thinking on emptiness were bricking up all of her time. She had written to her sister Christina about her preoccupation, Christina having gone through a rough patch around the time of her divorce. Christina had suggested this way out – if Sylvia didn't want another man, that is. So Sylvie had Annemarie call up the local parish priest, the Reverend Bernard Guthrie, a bachelor in his mid-thirties with a broad pink forehead and a full firm chin.

The first time Reverend Guthrie came round was for after-dinner coffee. The encounter left both Sylvie and the Reverend well pleased. As the hour passed, Sylvie was confirmed in her original impression of the young man as extremely presentable – serious and yet amiable. The Reverend was confirmed in his first deeply somatic impression of Sylvie's *Sachertorte*. He asked Sylvie for a second piece and after that an extra sliver. Sylvie pushed the cake plate over to his side of the table, liking him still more. She saw he was the kind of young man you might call Reverend Guthrie in deference to his vocation and the authority he represented; and then, after a few half-hours of acquaintance, ask about his family back home, his childhood, and talk about yourself, too.

'Reverend Guthrie,' she said, in the manner of an announcement, once she had picked the sticky crumbs off her skirt and called in Annemarie. 'You know I've asked you to come here today, in these difficult times of our loss, to help us with some doubts we've had.' She looked meaningfully at Annemarie, wishing that the girl had washed her hair and might close her legs.

'Mmm,' spoke the Reverend, struggling a little with the thickened throat that comes of eating *Sachertorte.*

'As I have explained, my late husband was not a man of faith. A good man, but not godly.'

The Reverend nodded encouragingly.

'Sadly, he did not believe in a life hereafter. But in the last few weeks, I have realised, speaking for myself, that I really want to believe. There must be something after this life. How else could it be?'

'Everlasting life was the gift of our Father,' the Reverend interjected.

'It must be so,' said Sylvie. 'We – ' She paused, glancing at Annemarie. 'We wanted you to come today to talk to us about this. My fear is that, lacking belief, John might now be lost. It's a terrible thought. Still, I would hope that, if he's out there, and if we believe, we may, all of us, be helped.' She spread her palms, facing upwards, on her knees in an effort to relax. She took a breath. She wished again that Annemarie might sit up, and sit more decently.

'The Father,' said Reverend Guthrie, delicately impaling a blotch of cream on his cake fork, 'through the agency of Jesus Christ, has ensured that we might all, all his children, have eternal life.'

'But,' said Annemarie, 'are we sure Father wanted it? Eternal life, that is.'

Sylvie snicked in her breath and pressed her palms together. But the Reverend was there to save her.

'We are not shown the mysteries of death,' he said, 'but it is my conviction that the loving kindness of the Father and of His Son will redeem the resistance of one who is no longer with us. Now it is important to give thanks where thanks are due. To recall our debts of gratitude. I would suggest that we pray.'

Though she tightened the grip of her hands, and crammed her lips together, Sylvie could not at first concentrate on the Reverend's prayer. She kept on seeing, through shut eyes, Annemarie's legs ajar, and the insolence in her slumped shoulders. What must the Reverend think? But there was no telling what the Reverend was thinking behind the mellifluous movement of his petitionary tongue.

'Guide our sisters,' he was murmuring. 'Give them solace, peace. You are Peace. You are Love.'

'He is Peace. He is Love,' Sylvie repeated after him, as he had earlier suggested she might. It was love that would save John, with a little of the Reverend's help. Love bringing them all peace. If she had not loved John enough before, she would love him now, in a more expanded and powerful way. She, too, would feel restored.

'Thank you, Reverend,' she said after the prayer had ended and they had remained silent together. 'Thank you. How can I ever thank you?'

She looked down at her hands, the lines red with the force of clenching. But she felt less anxious, that was sure. Annemarie had crossed her legs and was oscillating the pot, testing for more coffee. After she had gone to the kitchen, the Reverend handed Sylvie a new Bible, the New English. It crackled as she opened it. The Reverend said this Bible would make everything a lot more accessible to her. He also gave her a *Guidebook to Meaningful Prayer*, and a small poster, in the style of a sampler, which read: '——— ——— belongs to Jesus.' The Reverend instructed her to write her name in the space provided as soon as she felt able. At the end of each one of his sentences, Sylvie nodded. As he got up to leave, she took his hand in both of her own, and assured him she would do as he suggested. But he must come back soon.

'I'll come again, Mrs Rudolph, don't worry,' he said. 'We'll make it a regular date, until you feel strong. I just don't want you to worry about a thing. I will pray for you – you and your daughter.'

Sylvie swallowed hard. 'I am close to tears, Reverend,' she said.

As my father lay dying, I spent many hours thinking about our life after his death – the life Mother and I would share. I continued with these thoughts in my journal. My imaginings, looking forward to what seemed inconceivable, bore the deep rich gloss of fantasy. Lacking much experience of existence without the bounds of Merrydale – or, more strictly speaking, our house and garden, and the school – life beyond Father's death appeared as a timelessness of sisterly congeniality with Mother, an elaboration of the childhood picnics she had organised when I was younger – the butterfly cakes and jellied orange halves on coloured paper plates, the thermos cups filled with wilting cosmos – and also of her culture, by which I meant her piano playing, and her vocabulary of culinary terms. Mother sang to her own accompaniment and dispensed fondant sweetness; to live with her alone I might have everything of her: the companionship of a sort of Jane Eyre, and the refined company of Madame Merle.

*　　*　　*

But I got it a little wrong. It was not to be the first time. Father died. Mother went on to tranquillisers, stopped playing the piano, and grew fearful. For a while I was neither more nor less content than I had been before. I took up new topics in my journal. I wanted to devote time to the Big Questions of Life. Across the back blank pages of the book, I arranged certain important words in large sausage script. I wrote 'Meaning'; 'Reality'; 'Truth'. I spent several hours colouring these words in with some old wax crayons. 'Meaning' was in yellow with green stripes. Filling in the columns beneath each title, though, was less easy. I paged through a dictionary of quotations that had belonged to Father, found a yellowed piece of foolscap on which he too had once started to collect aphorisms, and gave up my own attempt.

Much of our existence went on just as before. Our home life was quiet; few people visited. To all intents and purposes, Mother and I were indeed each other's constant companions. As always, she made plenty of sweets and cakes. On Saturday mornings she washed out the Tupperware – the big tun-bellied bowls – and the cake tins, all of them deep, and lined each one with greaseproof paper. By Saturday night the Tupperware and the tins were full. But what was different now was that I no longer had a stomach for their contents. By now I was spending most of my allowance on Slenderettes.

Mother noticed I was getting thinner. She also said I was quieter than before; I was starting to worry her. Our daily talks after school over tea were impelled by a kind of panic.

'Tell me what happened today at school,' she might begin. 'I want to get the whole picture.'

She patted out a seat for me on the sofa beside her. She offered platefuls of treats.

'Here, have some of this fudge. I made it specially,' she coaxed. 'Don't you like it any more? Annemarie, little one, if there's something on your mind, you know you can tell your mother. You need never hesitate to come to me if you're troubled.'

'Yes, Mother, yes,' I said, taking the plate she offered and putting it back on the coffee table. 'Yes, I know I can come to you, but, no, everything is going well. No, no one asks me about Father any more. Yes, history is still my favourite subject. Last month we did the American Civil War; this week we are doing the Reformation in England.'

Mother's lips worked in sympathy with my own. She was leaning closer. Her eyes would be very near to mine. 'You are my life,' she whispered.

That was during the brief spring of 1976. Mother and I got used to a table set for two. At table Mother would often clasp my hand. Clasping my hand, she prayed before and after meals. She prayed also in the living-room before retiring at night, reading from the book the Reverend had given her. If I was in the living-room with her, she would ask me to join in, also reading from the book, but as I was spending more time in my bedroom, this did not happen very often. Looking in on me as she made her way to bed, Mother would tell me to think of my eyesight. What the two of us needed, she added, was our annual Christmas holiday.

It is noon at Tintagel, the Rudolphs' house. At such times, especially during the summer months when the sun is right overhead, the light has a flattening, abstracting effect. Bulk dissolves; hard surfaces tremble. The bungalow seems to lose substance. The wire gauze in the hailscreens glitters, blurs, forming a band that stretches lengthwise across the house like a mirage. The lawn, lush, silver, unbroken by flowerbeds, holds a mirror to the sky. An abandoned spade, a coiled hosepipe, Simon's woollen hat, are smudges in the effulgent space.

At such times there seems to be only the music; the music saturates the light with sound. Sylvie likes to listen to Schubert's last sonatas as she works in the kitchen. The record player is in the living-room, so when Annemarie is not at home she has the music on loud. If it is very hot, or the house feels very quiet, she plays the music so loud that the Chinese brass vases ring. Sometimes, if she knows that Annemarie will not be back for a while, she stops her work, draws the curtains, sits back in the sofa and closes her eyes. When the music plays, she feels only the music: she is aware neither of sorrow nor of heat.

By Christmas of the year of John's death, Sylvie was reserving Saturday afternoons between five and six for tea talks with the Reverend. In the dying heat of the day the two sat together on the verandah, backed up against the hailscreens. She would have her knitting, he his pipe. Sylvie had begun by tempting him with the delicacies that Annemarie was refusing, but before long she was baking with him in mind. She had the manager at the Merrydale Superette order ingredients he had never heard of before: kirsch and halva and cardamom, angelica and walnut butter. Every Friday she scanned her cookery books for new recipes and every Saturday she was busy in the kitchen till almost five.

But the Reverend never disappointed her. He beamed beneficently upon the spread on the table between them. He insisted, no matter how often Sylvie clapped her apron to her mouth in bewilderment, to say grace over her fine baking. He took the apron from her hands. Truly, he was a gentleman: not only a good and reverent man, but a gentleman, combining sensitivity with manners.

As on the very first occasion of their meeting, they ended each afternoon with a communal prayer.

'Father whom we honour,' the Reverend began. 'For what we have received . . . '

And 'Amen, Amen,' Sylvie punctuated his words.

Towards the end the Reverend joined in. 'Amen,' he pronounced, in decisive tones. And then again, on a low note, 'Amen,' the sound lingering against his palate.

'Ah, Ah-men,' Sylvie agreed, edging in the word. 'Amen.'

Then, finally, fixedly staring at each other, their torsos rigid with the intensity of their emotion, taking in breath at the same moment, 'Amen,' on a falling tone.

They dropped their eyes after that. Sylvie would sigh a little, ruminatively, and the Reverend would tap his pipe against his patella. He left soon afterwards, never forgetting his promise to come again – yes, at five o'clock – next week.

It was because of the Reverend's visits that Sylvie booked a shorter summer holiday for herself and Annemarie that year. In previous years they had spent the last week of December and the first week of January at a mountain resort called Dragon Peak, set against the verdant river valley slope of a butte. It had been John's treat to her each year, a holiday alone with her daughter. He himself claimed that he had no need for holiday breaks; honestly speaking, he said, mountain altitudes made him nauseous. He drove them out to Dragon Peak, and, two weeks later, picked them up again.

'Have you had a good holiday?' he asked them each time, simultaneously tipping the porter with one hand, and locking Sylvie and Annemarie into the car with the other.

'Yes, Father, yes, John, yes,' they chorused. 'Yes. Thank you so much.'

*　　*　　*

34

This year was the first time that Sylvie was to drive out alone. It was also the first time, she had to admit to herself, that she was not looking forward to the holiday with all of her usual end-of-year excitement. That she and Annemarie needed to be away from the house for a while was certain. But Sunday to Sunday fortnight also meant two whole weeks without the Reverend. The thought made her nervous. She suggested to Annemarie that they cut their time in the mountains by half. When this healing period was done and she no longer needed to see the Reverend as often, then they could take a longer holiday. Annemarie offered no objection. 'Yes, Mother, yes. All right,' she said.

At Dragon Peak Resort city people with some money to spare gathered for exercises in robust relaxation. They were housed in thatched rondavel huts in the African style, clustered close, also in the African manner, to suggest the proximity of the African wild and the open veld. To counterbalance this, to give the effect of home away from home, a team of waiters was employed to hasten from hut to hut, from dawn to post-dinner dance, bearing stainless steel trays of beverages and light comestibles. The resort was situated in a baboon and eland game park. At a distance of about twenty miles from its centre, the park was surrounded everywhere by a high barbed-wire fence that climbed the valley sides and wriggled along butte edges. The fence served – it was well advertised at the hotel – to keep in the animals, and to protect the guests.

Sylvie and Annemarie booked into the hut John had always chosen for them, the one closest to the dining-room, close enough to save Sylvie's perm, moulded the day before leaving home, should it storm at dinner-time. The rondavel room was large, with a view out on to the right side of the Dragon butte and most of the river valley. There were two beds, separated by a bedside table, as in the master bedroom at home. The bedspread design, like that of the floor-covering and the wallpaper, was a chorus-line profusion of pink feathers. To the outside was a stable door, enhancing the effect of the country; between the room and the bathroom *en suite* hung a white plastic shower curtain, sprinkled with blue guppies. On entering the familiar room that year, Annemarie wondered, as she had the year before, how she might spend a week without her journal. It was a book Sylvie refused to pack.

But Sylvie was proficient at filling up their time. She set her alarm for six-thirty each morning. By that time the sun had already edged some way down the valley slope, and a tea tray waited on the doorstep. While they had tea in bed, Sylvie read aloud from the Bible and prayed; the Reverend had set her reading for the week. Their breakfast, up in the main dining-room, was extended, copious, multi-tiered. Sylvie liked to arrive early and to leave late. For the one occasion of the year that she had the opportunity, she wanted to see what was being worn in the city. The pants suits were more tailored this year, she noticed; metal belts were in. Annemarie should have a look at the woman passing on her left: hemlines were starting to come down, which was a huge improvement in the way of style.

Sylvie and Annemarie devoted each day to vigorous, healthy activity: to tennis and bowls and ramblings along the river valley. The evenings they spent preparing for dinner, a process which usually took up more time than morning orisons. Sylvie would tend to Annemarie's rough bits – elbows, knees and feet – with a loofah and cream. Annemarie sprayed Sylvie's perfume for her just where Sylvie liked it, but where it was difficult to reach – on the flat of her shoulder blades and on the bump of bone at the base of her neck. Each dinner-time they sat in virtual silence, Annemarie facing the wall and Sylvie the other guests.

'Just look at all these people,' was Sylvie's general murmur over coffee. 'How many clothes they must have to be able to change three times a day. How I would love to have a peek at their wardrobes.'

That year, perhaps because she found her mind wandering during dinner or morning prayers, Annemarie became infatuated with the middle-aged man who occupied the rondavel next to theirs. On their third day, she had stopped to admire his hiking boots. The boots were sturdy, built up high to grip the ankles. Annemarie began to keep watch on the man. The bathroom window of their rondavel conveniently faced on to his front door-step. She discovered he spent much of his time sitting on a grass mat on the step, reading. When he looked up, Annemarie could make believe he was looking back at her.

On the fifth day of their holiday, watered and soaped, Sylvie and Annemarie encountered their neighbour on their way to dinner. He fell in step with them. He smelt, Annemarie thought, of grass and sun. Sylvie, swallowing a grimace, thought of a clean shirt pulled over a sweaty body. She situated herself beside the tall bony column of the man's arm and shoulder.

'We've been impressed by all the reading material we see lying out on your door-step,' she remarked.

'Really,' said their neighbour, missing the appropriate interrogative inflection. 'They are adventure stories, holiday reading.'

'Annemarie, here, is also a reader,' Sylvie went on. 'When we come to the mountains, though, we tend to spend most of our time out of doors walking. This place is so healthy; you want to make the most of it.'

Their neighbour's lips tightened in what could have been a nasal monosyllabic had he made the effort to produce the sound. Annemarie, blushing deeply, restrained herself from invoking her mother's name. There was silence between the three of them. They approached the dining-room.

'Ah, the dining-room,' said Sylvie.

Their neighbour nodded at them, to right and far right, and moved off rapidly.

'One of those readers,' said Sylvie in a voice of mild reproof.

Later that night their neighbour was joined by two friends, two women, on his front door-step. Their laughter, from where Annemarie lay in bed, seemed frequent and easy. She listened until they said goodbye. Her mother, Annemarie saw, was long asleep. She watched her lying hunched up on her side. She looked strangely small. Annemarie shifted a little closer, wanting to catch her breathing.

On their last night, the sixth, as a treat, Sylvie and Annemarie had their after-dinner coffees out on the red-clay verandah which flanked the dining-room, instead of inside with the other guests. A waiter in black tie brought the coffee tray. Sylvie tipped him with a flourish, allowing the coins to rattle noisily on the tray. She finished her coffee before Annemarie. She rolled her chocolate mint papers into tight balls, rubbed at a speck on her collar, then said she might go and settle the bill so they could have an early start in the morning. She would see Annemarie at the hut in a quarter of an hour.

It was one of the first times that holiday that Annemarie found herself alone. She sat with her hands in her lap. She tried to commit to memory all that she should record in her journal. The facts kept slipping from her mind. She looked up and saw that their neighbour had joined her on the verandah. He was sitting several tables away, smiling over at her. Though her lips seemed difficult to control, she smiled back.

'Like to go on an outing tomorrow?' he asked.

Annemarie knew she could make no verbal response. She shifted about in her chair, tried crossing her legs, then uncrossed them again.

'We go with the game warden along the boundary fence. To check for places where poachers have broken in.'

'We're leaving tomorrow,' Annemarie said, only half regretfully. 'And I think we might have trouble keeping up.'

The man shifted forwards in his chair, as though he wanted to come closer. He was slightly frowning, showing regret, but continued to smile. 'I was hoping you could have come alone,' he said. 'Reconnoitering can be fun.'

That did it. With that remark Annemarie resolved to fix his image in her mind. She was impressed. Was it not an impressive invitation? She saw the two of them in khaki creeping through the long veld grass. She could imagine resting under protea bushes with him, watching sun splashes through the leaves.

'What tick bit you, I wonder?' asked Sylvie on the way home the next day, periodically swerving towards the kerb in her efforts to peruse Annemarie's profile. 'I'll have to check the skin on your back and legs in the bath tonight, to make sure that nothing got you. Ticks find the oddest spots.'

Annemarie did not reply. She was composing a new set of entries for her journal.

For the greater part of 1977, or at least up until the period of our mock final exams at school, I was infatuated with a man whom we met on holiday, whose name I no longer know and may never have known. His face draws a blank in my mind. I have no idea why I first noticed him. What I remember is what I felt, and what I felt was love. In my writing I repeatedly told myself I was in love. Being in love provided new material for my journal. I spent even more time writing than before, and writing now offered more pleasure than I had ever imagined possible. Episode after exciting episode was unreeling so quickly in my mind that I began to work on several simultaneously, beginning them five pages apart, shuttling rapidly between them. 'Love and Dust', one may have been called, 'Mountain Storm' another. The veld patroller and I kept watch at border fences, living rough, outwitting strong predators, sharing water mouth to mouth, enduring. I wrote with my left hand jammed firmly between my thighs. I forgot the time.

'Annemarie, it's eleven,' Mother called from the kitchen where she was tidying up and mopping the floor.

'Mother, I'm writing.'

'Annemarie, come on. It's time to stop. You're ruining both your eyes and your health,' Mother said a little later, coming over and placing my cup of warm milk and honey squarely on the page in front of me.

I stopped writing anywhere but in my bedroom. I took my journal to bed to reread it. I transported myself and my hero off to the desert and down the untamed tropical coast. I foraged through the novels at the newsagent's for new ideas. I observed how much more gripping my own story was than these. The saga went into four volumes, four hardcover narrow-ruled books.

I spent 1977 on a personal African exploration in a hormonal daze. Beneath the dates of that year, needlessly marked at the top of the narrow-ruled pages in black ink, I imagined ways of being adult. Nothing else was important. The months passed: Mother became friendlier with the Church, at some stage she was baptised; the Reverend visited regularly; at school, teachers spoke the word revision. I wrote. I wrote without an ear for my mother's pleas. I wrote and caught myself smiling fixed in the reflection of the darkened window, between the partly closed curtains. I was still writing on the day that a newspaper was unfolded in front of me and the date revealed. That was in September '77. In September '77, though my writing went on for a few more months, my African adventure ended.

It can be said that I was a seventies adolescent. But only because I grew up in the seventies. I had no sense of the present, and only a vague theoretical notion that time was passing. As I grew up, somewhere, quite close, but elsewhere, there was a generation in foment that came to be known as the generation of '76. In 1976 I was sixteen, in 1977, seventeen, but that seventies generation was not mine. In a certain way, you could say, I did not know where in time or space I was.

It was an agreement between Sylvie and the Reverend that they would continue with their Saturday afternoon meetings until such time as Sylvie began to feel less perturbed. With the problem of Annemarie, though, that time was indefinitely postponed. Worry was no longer the word for her concern about her daughter. What she felt was a nagging distress. Annemarie was not acting as she should – not in the least. She neither ate nor spoke; she did not go out of doors. She did not menstruate very regularly, as Sylvie could judge from the sanitary towels left in the bathroom, but still she looked anaemically pale. Blue veins stretched taut across her bones. No teenager acts the way they should, the Reverend told her; but Sylvie was not convinced. With

Annemarie, she said, it was different: Annemarie was too strange.

The compulsive writing that she did was the worst of it. Were it not for that, Annemarie was sure to come round and rouse herself sometime. But the writing stood in the way of everything; she wrote instead of eating and instead of talking. Sylvie was sure she sometimes forgot to bath. She must transcribe every thought she had into that tiny millipede script. How else could she keep at it, continuously, every night of every day?

Annemarie had of course always been a little writer. There was even a time, that dear round-cheeked time, when Annemarie had shown all that she wrote to Sylvie. She had written page-long poems called 'My Garden' and 'I Like . . . ' She read them aloud to Sylvie. Beating time, Sylvie had helped her to make the rhythm sing – ta-tum, ta-tum. But Annemarie no longer wrote poetry, or said she did not. In this Sylvie was inclined to believe her. She doubted that Annemarie's mind tended towards tripping rhymes and pretty motifs. Sylvie had seen – it had been inadvertent, she was so fraught – what Annemarie had written in her journal at the time of her father's death. It was after they had given Sylvie the tranquillisers. She was lying on the sofa in the hospital waiting-room. Annemarie had just walked out the door. Sylvie had asked her, please, hug your mother. But Annemarie had not replied.

'I'm going to order tea,' she had called.

Sylvie turned on to her side. The journal was open on the ashtray stand. She did not really want to look. It was the repeat pattern in the writing that drew her eye, the obscene neatness of it: 'My father is dead, my father is dead.' Written over and over, the words were built into a column erected down the page.

The Reverend, when she told him of this, said everyone

needs outlets. Each person has their own way of coping with pain. Even so, Sylvie thought, outlets need not stay permanently open; wounds heal. John died more than a year ago. What more could Annemarie find to say on the topic? The way the child was going, she would write her life into that book. Sylvie got a queasy feeling at the thought. She was reminded of gargoyle pictures she had once seen in a photo book on Europe: oversized fishes with prominent fins and widestaring eyes craning all the way round to swallow their tails.

Sylvie continued to try to distract Annemarie.

'Annemarie,' she said, standing at her daughter's bedroom door one warm afternoon, 'my small Annemarie. Don't you have something else to do? A friend to see? Get out into the sun. It's not too bad outside today, not too hot. Or simply come and spend time with your mother. We could listen to some music. I could teach you how to knit.'

Annemarie started, blinked, sat with her fists balled on either side of her book, the pen clamped like a spoon.

'Not right now, Mother. I'm busy writing.'

'But, little one, you're always always writing. What do you find to say?'

'I don't always write about what I do. I write about other things.'

'What kind of things? Tell your mother. Annemarie, don't shut me out. Show me so that I can understand.' Sylvie held out her hands. 'Here, show me what you're writing, just like you used to do.'

Annemarie folded her arms across the page. 'It's my own writing, Mother,' she said. 'And it's my own time that I take up with writing. I like to do it.'

'I know,' said Sylvie. 'That's part of my worry.'

*   *   *

43

Once Sylvie called the mother of a classmate of Annemarie's. The child seemed to have no friends – or none she brought home, anyway – but Elise Lovemore she occasionally telephoned about homework. She had left the number on the telephone pad, so Sylvie phoned Mrs Lovemore. Because she had Annemarie's interests at heart, she had no difficulty finding the words to say.

'My daughter is closed to me. I live alone in the house,' she told Mrs Lovemore.

Mrs Lovemore clicked her tongue and made reference to the times they were living in. 'The children are under stress,' she said.

From the Reverend, Sylvie found out where the Lovemores lived. She drove past the house one day. A stripped car hulk and a lopsided junglegym drifted in an overgrown lawn. She resolved to ignore Mrs Lovemore's words.

But she was less able to dismiss the Reverend's advice easily. Especially because it was so sweet to be soothed by him. The Reverend too tried to look for compromises. He found ways of distracting her from her worries without dismissing them. He would agree that Annemarie was not behaving even as a particularly reclusive adolescent might, and then matched with anecdotes of his own each example of estranged behaviour that Sylvie could quote in the course of a Saturday afternoon. He spoke of similar symptoms observed in other households – closed doors, darkened rooms, loss of appetite. As he spoke Sylvie was quiet with the force of concentration. Then when he finished she would enumerate exceptions.

'But never to speak, even at meal-times?' she pointed out. 'To eat only white bread and biscuits from one day end to another? To sit with the electric light on all day? And also the sitting, just sitting, all day long? It's not natural, Reverend, not natural at all. No wonder her sweat smells bad.'

'But these are hard times for her,' said the Reverend. 'Perhaps her system is reacting.'

'She's unhealthy, Reverend,' Sylvie went on. 'The sweat on her smells of stale tea and anger. When I smell it my worry grows. What am I to do with that child? When she was little she was not like this.'

Towards the end of the afternoon the Reverend would suggest that it was best simply to pray. If Sylvie sat unmoved, he tried to distract her attention.

'Look, Mrs Rudolph,' he said one afternoon in August, pointing with his lips because his hands were occupied with a butterfly cake and the *Guidebook to Meaningful Prayer*, 'imagine it. It will soon be spring again. Spring may mean exam time for the children, but it's time also for new beginnings.'

Sylvie was looking out at the burnished brown glaze of the dry lawn. The hills and surrounding farmlands were barred in black. It was the season of veld fires. Each night the hills were crisscrossed with streaks of flame. When the wind blew, it brought with it ash and the brittle parings of charred grass roots.

'I look forward to the spring,' she said.

'It seems to me,' said the Reverend, 'that you could make the most of it if you gave your garden some more colour. Have Simon do a flowerbed right in the middle of the lawn there. A round bed. Fill it with bright flowers. Make a big bright sun. Simon can do it for you.'

Sylvie followed with her eyes the jabbing motions of his cake.

'It might be an idea,' she said.

Two weeks later the Reverend presented her with a potted amaryllis to commemorate the new seasonal year.

'This is a token of the coming spring,' he said. 'Of God's creation, and of my appreciation of our friendship.'

Sylvie dimpled.

'Things will feel better in the spring, Reverend,' she agreed.

Sylvie was to frame that particular tea in her memory. Because of what the Reverend said that day, the afternoon would always appear to her as a very special time. After she had taken the amaryllis from him, the Reverend advised her on placing it in the living-room. Then she went off to pop a lemon meringue pie into the oven for a few moments: the Reverend liked his slightly warm. When she appeared with the pie, he came forward to take it from her, smiling, his arms outstretched. And after that they moved to their places on the verandah. Not saying very much for a while, they watched Simon chisel out the border of the new flowerbed. The mynahs were raucous overhead. From far away came the sound of voices singing, a chant wafted to and fro on the breeze, blown over from the township across the hills.

Annemarie called Simon round to fetch his food. Sylvie commented that Annemarie might forget this duty too, the making of Simon's lunch, if she was not reminded, over and over. The Reverend raised a cautionary hand.

'Mrs Rudolph,' he said, 'praise be that there is food for all of us; food to give to Simon, regardless of Annemarie's reluctance; food also, this wonderful weekly feast, for me. We must keep reminding ourselves how good it is to have it, how thankful we are, how glad to be here.'

'Yes, I'm glad,' Sylvie nodded.

'I'm certainly glad to be here, Mrs Rudolph. I'm very happy . . . ' He sat down hard against the back of his chair to make his point. 'Very glad to be needed here,' he repeated. 'It makes me feel at home.'

Sylvie arrested her nodding on a downward motion. She was flattered. Her chin was tucked in and her eyes were lowered. She had to bite her lip.

'I'm glad you feel needed here, Reverend,' she said.

*   *   *

It was after this that Sylvie began to feel she should make an effort to improve her home. The point was that if the Reverend was glad to visit, she must do what she could to keep him feeling that way. He had given her a lead with the suggestion about the flowerbed. She should now try to gladden his eye. Setting up tasks to do, she would also be filling time while Annemarie was shut away with her books. The examinations were coming closer, so Sylvie would be even lonelier than before. But if she also had a project to complete, and a pretty house to show for it, then, by Christmas, wouldn't they both deserve their holiday? They could go somewhere different; not the mountains this time but somewhere very relaxing, a convivial place where they could be close and quite together, as a mother and her daughter should.

Sylvie began by refurbishing the living-room. The curtains still hung heavy with the yellow scale of John's smoking. Bringing them down was like removing the last of him. But then she'd meant to change them for years. She called in a professional decorator, a woman in court shoes from Hoopstad, the nearest city, who plucked at the curtain fringes, the cushion tassles and the grime-cured antimacassars, saying they all had to go. Sylvie phoned her broker, who said her portfolio looked unshakeable, so she agreed with the decorator.

Sylvie chose a dusty gold selection: linen for the upholstery and long soft drapes. She bought a new carpet – woven wool giving a clotted-cream effect – and a pouffe in springbok hide – to blend in with the dusty gold. Above the fireplace, instead of the Karoo landscape by the foot-and-mouth artist they'd had for years, she hung a long oval mirror in a gilt frame. The frame had been moulded to form sun rays, creating the impression – almost, Sylvie thought – of a Bernini altar. Above her favourite chair, oddly bereft of cushions, she hung an enlargement of a black-and-white picture of John, taken in his early thirties, long before she ever knew him. She liked it, though – it showed him in a particularly good light. When she had hung the picture, her final touch, she took the time to sit in her chair and admire the new effect. She had worked quickly: she was proud. The hailscreens alone did not blend in. She no longer consciously saw the chicken wire, but the pine slats, she noticed, were unsanded and bare. So she had Simon smooth them down and paint them white. That way you really could hardly see them, even from the outside.

The day the Reverend complimented Sylvie on her improved living-room, she discovered a new confidence. Unless you change a little – she now saw it so clearly – you don't realise how a house can become a museum to the past and hold you there. You grow stale. In the storage space under the roof beams Sylvie stacked the boxes of antimacassars, curtains and stripped upholstery. She decided to get out more, to see what was happening in Merrydale and to keep feeling interested.

The previous year a new shopping centre had opened on the outskirts of town, the first of its kind in the district. It was built around a pedestrian walkway in yellow-brick herring-bone. On either side of the walkway was a row of small shops. You could spend many pleasant hours – Mrs Roberts too had said it. The centre was on the opposite side of town from the bus depot and the Indian shops, where the crowds were thick and black. You need have no fear here as a white woman; the centre was European and civilised.

Each time Sylvie went she would stop first at the American Star doughnut stand and each time she would try to choose a doughnut different from the one she had had before. This was the first time in her life that she had ever tried doughnuts. She chose the ones with the stickiest inner rings, so she could eat all the way around the outside, and then take the inside in gulps. If she had courage, she would buy an extra one for Annemarie, but, as Annemarie usually refused the gift, she would then save it for herself, to eat in bed after she had switched off the light. Once Sylvie bought one for the Reverend: double chocolate icing, and a thick mat of coconut and pink vermicelli. She made a trip home specially to get greaseproof wrapping and left the doughnut in his letterbox.

The doughnuts were to whet her appetite. After that she visited the shops. In the chemist you could test new perfumes and creams, and, sometimes, if you bought enough cream, you might get a free gift. In the food store they handed out egg-cup portions of new products – cheese dip, guava sandwich paste, new spicy *wors*. Sylvie tried each one. The whole place gave you a sense of overseas; it really showed the country was moving on, despite what rumourmongers said. It was the glossiness and polish, the plate glass and freshly painted signs. Seeing it all, you were tempted to redo the whole of your home. Sylvie bought more bits and pieces: a fluffy taupe toilet set complete with an ornamental holder for the extra roll; a new dressing-table stool, in wrought iron and prim pink satin – looking as though it might have come straight out of an Edwardian tea garden; and a door-knocker, an elongated brass drop, shaped very like a knobkerrie.

With each purchase, Sylvie felt more secure. It is remarkable – she repeatedly told the Reverend to emphasise how she was improving under his care – it is really quite remarkable how much better you feel when you try for something different. She started buying the *Merrydale Herald* to find out what was happening in town. She read about local touch-rugby events, main street road works, the dangers of rabid dogs in the Merrydale area; also about the social functions – bonanza charity *braais*, prize jam-and-marmalade fairs, mid-morning prayer groups – the sort of events that the Reverend might be attending in his capacity as an important town personality. She gathered conversation points for when she had to wait in queues at tills. During till conversations and in the *Herald* she heard about the Merrydale History Society. She heard the Society was very active and covered a great deal of ground; that there was a lot to learn. She decided to join. She would have more to tell the Reverend on Saturdays.

The Merrydale History Society, Sylvie discovered, busied itself with weekly talks by local specialists and monthly visits to places of interest. There were enough of these historical spots around. The gentle undulations of the surrounding land had scooped up as offerings for the hereafter many distressed and expatriated souls. Sylvie had been unaware of this before – the new highways running down to the coast skirted these empty tracts of thorn tree and grass. Yet, if you knew where to look – if, with a sweep and clutch of his pink hand, Mr Reg Dimbleby re-created this brave British onslaught, that clash – you could see that the land was loaded with time. There were residual remains everywhere, not so much of the kingdoms before the white man came – those kraals of mud and straw – but signs rather of the effort and struggle of the courageous pioneers: the scar of ox wagon wheel in rock, tumbled cairns of whitewashed *klip*, short cenotaphs stabbing the broad sky. Catching her daughter sidling into or out of her bedroom, Sylvie said Annemarie should open her curtains wide and imagine for herself all the history that must have unfolded out there on the veld. Think of the lines of sturdy ox wagons in the wake of the blacks, the stalwart Scottish farmers come to fructify the land, the Redcoats on the march to make an Empire secure.

'Later, Mother,' said Annemarie, looking intently down the

passage or over her shoulder, at her desk. 'For the time being I have European history to do.'

With the late spring in Merrydale, before the onset of the long summer, comes an evanescence of tender clear light. For a few days the distant hills seem to draw closer. Their outlines are precise. In the morning, dew lingers only in the deepest shadow. The jasmine in the old Victorian graveyard and the hawthorn trees running down the centre of Main Street bloom briefly, are pruinose. This year the History Society decides to cancel two of its monthly outings because of veld fires: battleground contours have been blotted out by blackness; the ladies would smudge their slacks. Instead, garden tours are organised. Many of the ladies have large and splendid gardens. On each occasion, tea is served at about four, perhaps out on the lawn or perhaps on the covered patio, depending on the inclination of the hostess. Mrs Rudolph, a new Society member, does not miss a single garden tour.

In the rapid spring of 1977 the amaryllis given to Mrs Rudolph by the Reverend Guthrie stands in a side window niche in the living-room. This is the right place for it; it is centred, framed. The long-limbed stalks reach up; the two heavy blooms face outwards. At a squint the effect is of a bather, rising out of water, stretching up, hands and arms extended. Mrs Rudolph, letting her knitting drop into her lap, likes to look at the plant against the light, to think about the solicitude of the man who bestowed it. She knows she will always be grateful to him.

It is from the outside, though, despite the reflections in the glass and the obscuring screens, that the amaryllis is shown off to its best effect. The colours stand out, the crimson freaked with saffron and shadow. Whenever she is out in the garden, Mrs Rudolph pauses to gaze at the plant from this side also. Again she admires its handsomeness, the regal reach of the blooms. It is its singleness, there in the window frame, that makes the perfect picture. Despite the season, one would not place the plant out of doors. Where it stands is exactly right.

PART TWO

I have said that in the month of September 1977 my African romance ended. Eight months I spent telling myself that story, then one day I turned to the next empty page in my journal and could think of no way of filling it: I had lost the point – or maybe the joy – of the writing. What happened I think now was that I had caught the sense of another story – though one I yet had no way of setting to words – and this idea of a new story blocked the old. So I lacked the means of expression not because, in that well-known way they have, the words were intractable and would not add up to make sentences. It was all a lot simpler and then again a lot more difficult than that. The problem, you see, was not one of words at all. I was being teased by the feeling that something – almost here, just here, appearing any minute – had to be told, but I could not yet imagine quite what it could be. Sitting around, waiting for what might emerge, I found I no longer had much to say.

The way things turned out, I was to abandon the journal long before any sort of new story could develop. It could well be that in the spaces I then left open I have started to write the words that appear here. Because I was not at that time telling as many tales, because I was spending more time away from my journal, I am able now to remember more of what happened; and because I remember more, though I lack the books themselves, I am able from this point on to present a fuller account. I see the events more clearly because they appear without an overlay of words.

I am even able to put a precise date to the time things started to change. It was 17 September 1977: the day I received an item of information I could not at once transfer to my journal. It did not fit in with anything I had been doing up to that time. That day I first began to suspect that the story which had formed the primary substance of my existence might from now on resist telling. I tried hard to keep the two together, the narrative and experience. As I have explained, I was used to keeping my journal account flush with my life. I wanted to translate my new concerns directly into the journal and so I copied reports word for word from the pages of the newspaper and transcribed interviews, response for response. Leaders and feature articles I saved and pasted in directly – the back pages of the journal were hardened with glue. But, despite all my efforts, I was never very sure that this method worked. More than simply wedging the hard evidence of my reading deep into my journal, and remembering and then rehearsing dates and names, what I wanted was to know the material, to have it in my possession as though it were in fact part of my life.

As the months passed I began to find it more and more difficult to continue with the exercise. This is why, when the final break came, it was not as startling as you might expect. I had been waiting for an intervention because I couldn't put an end to the journal myself. I could not forbid my own words. Or perhaps everything was a lot simpler than that; perhaps it was not so much the anticipation of a new story that stopped me as that it was impossible to spend all my time writing. In that Mother may have been right. What I now began to want was – not to cease from writing, not to close up the journal for good – perhaps merely to do something else. The only hitch – slight, perhaps, but real – was that, unlike in the pages of my journal, the events that happened outside of it were not subject to the control of my pen.

17 September 1977: it was a day marked by an ordinary encounter. Nothing in it, really, just looking at it – two people speaking (except that it was the first time they had spoken); and the showing of the photograph, of the man I had never heard of before.

As always on a Saturday – Mother being busy with the Reverend and tea – I made Simon's five o'clock meal. I did it, as always, only after she had pointedly called my name from the verandah to remind me. Writing in my bedroom, I easily forgot the time. I cut, again as usual, the four thick slices of brown bread, thick enough to stop a hasty mouth. I spread them, first with white margarine – the yellow being for Mother and me alone – then with peanut butter mixed together with watermelon jam. The peanut butter and jam, too, were especially for Simon, bought for him in bulk at the end of each half-year and kept on his own bit of kitchen shelf.

I spread the bread meticulously, right into the corners, because I knew from the school lunches Mother made that crusts need extra attention. Sitting at my desk and staring out at the hailscreens, limning sentences and hyperbolic curves against the chicken wire, it had struck me that Simon might like softened crusts. It seemed, if I looked closely, that he was working quite hard out there in the heat. The sandwiches, cut into two to make fist-filling chunks, I handed to Simon on one of the week's newspapers folded into four. Then I proffered his black 'Our Dad' mug, in which three tea bags were stewing, with the other hand.

The moment of exchange was invariably tricky. Mugs have a way of radiating heat. Balancing newspaper and sandwiches on the inside of his forearm, Simon would gingerly take the rim of the mug as I swivelled the handle round to meet his free hand. Without catching each other's eyes – we were concentrating on not spilling the hot liquid – we rarely missed the small drama. If it was successfully accomplished we would both smile absent-mindedly at each other's toes; if it was not, if tea spilled, we would flick our fingers and chuckle briefly in a shamefaced kind of way, still avoiding one another's eyes.

On this particular September day, though, Simon forgot the ritual. The newspaper had his attention the moment I handed him the sandwiches. He let out his breath noisily, in a kind of whistle. As he took the paper, his grasp as firm and exact as usual, one finger was already pointing.

He said, 'It's him.'

We had never spoken before. I was taken aback.

'What?' I said. 'Who?'

He took the mug from me, placed it on the kitchen door-step and, holding the paper, shifted the sandwiches to one side, precisely, as I remember it, with the back of a flat hand.

He pointed to the picture on the front page. It was a photograph of a charcoal-sketch portrait – of a man. The man was looking to one side, his lips just slightly smiling.

'It is Steve,' he said.

'Steve?' I asked.

He did not reply at once. He was looking at the portrait.

With an impatience I clearly remember, a feeling of 'so what is it you know?', I again asked, 'Steve? Steve who?'

His eyes were fixed on mine, their expression impassive. I

had to look away. I took the sandwiches and balanced them on the mug standing on the step.

'It is Stephen Biko. Our man,' he said as I straightened up again.

I was lost for something to say. Because I had never doubted that being white I should be in the know about things, it was uncomfortable to reveal – very clearly to reveal – that I wasn't. My chin developed a widespread itch, but I did not give way to scratching. I felt Simon was still staring across at me.

Finally I asked, 'So who is Steve Biko, then?'

'Hey man, you must read the papers,' said Simon.

Though he did not laugh, I heard mockery in his words. I thought for a moment of Father. When they grow up and get cheeky we must tell them go, Father had remarked many times when speaking on the subject of garden labour. Still, I wanted to find out what it was Simon knew. It was quite absurd that he was in charge of facts entirely obscure to me. I took a step forward, out the door, off the step.

'I do read the news,' I said, 'but mainly the international stuff.'

Simon finally laughed. He simultaneously took a step backwards to maintain the space between us.

'Look,' he said, unfolding the paper, stretching and cracking it along the creases with the hands of one practised, 'see here.'

The picture now appeared with its caption. It was simply the name: Bantu Stephen Biko.

'This is our man. They killed him.'

'Who killed him?' I asked.

He laughed again but the laugh seemed of a different quality. Father, had he been listening, would by now be glowering, angered by the short harsh call of the laugh, and equally by the silence that followed. Maintaining the silence,

Simon carefully refolded the paper along its former crease marks and held his hand out for the food. I picked up the mug. The sandwiches were still balancing on it. I noticed the bread was soggy from catching the steam.

'I can keep it? The paper?' Simon then said.

'Do you want it, to read?' I asked inanely. I think I wanted to delay him, maybe to hear more.

'You want it?'

'I'd like to read it.'

'OK. But next week you must give it to me.'

He smoothed the paper, then placed it on the step in order to take the mug from me. The sandwiches he grasped as a clump. As the tea had cooled, the handing-over this time was simple. I picked up the paper. I noticed that the sand and wet off his hand had puckered the picture where the buttered bread had moistened it. The moment of our exchange, I thought to myself, was marked into the ink.

Now, from the verandah, Mother was hailing me. I had taken longer than usual performing my afternoon task. Did I need help? she called.

Simon and I both looked hastily towards the door. I thought Mother might send Reverend Guthrie to see what was going on. I moved back inside. Stealthily high-stepping, glancing from me to his mug to the door, Simon backed off. He again exaggerated his care carrying the tea, as though it was still hot. Just as he disappeared around the corner he caught my eye. We did not smile, but perhaps we nodded – or again, perhaps we didn't. However it was I felt we shared a sort of greeting – an understanding that I was here, being called at, and not with the other two on the verandah.

'Mother, I've given Simon his food,' I called back.

That was 17 September. The next Saturday, while Mother was still at the hairdresser preparing for tea with the Reverend,

I went out to where Simon was mulching, to give him the paper. I had set out without thinking, but when I brought myself up beside him and he went on working – his back stretching and flexing at the spine-base and the sweat rich upon it – I wished I had thought out beforehand what to say. I half-heartedly held out the paper. As he did not turn, I let my arm fall. I watched his hands delve and smooth, delve and smooth. I wondered how it must be to work like this on Saturdays, every Saturday, and go to school for the rest of the week. Mother said he did go to school – indeed, that he must. I looked back at the house, at the densely enmeshed hutch of my bedroom window. I wondered whether it was possible for him to see me sitting there.

'Simon,' I said. It was the first time that I had spoken the name instead of calling it out for meal-time summonses. He straightened up and turned to face me, blowing his lips. I felt his sweat on my face. I involuntary followed him in wiping off my forehead with the back of my wrist. The paper was in the hand thus raised, so I did not need to hold it out again. As we brought our arms down, he took it from me. I expected him to speak. He did not.

Standing in silence, I began to feel that the sun was very hot, and that the close points of my body, my belly creases and armpits, were crawling with moisture. I shrugged inside my long-sleeved dress. It had seemed appropriate in my bedroom, where it was dim. Simon too nudged his shoulders against his neck, breaking and spreading the beads of sweat. I was vaguely aware of being put out – the way we parted last week seemed to have promised an easier opening. I also perceived he would again start to work if I did not first speak.

'Can you tell me a bit about this man Biko?' I said, forming the syllables rapidly, for I thought that my increasing awkwardness would make me mash them together.

'It is in the paper,' he said.

'But you could also tell me something of what you know?'
I said. I recognised somewhere in my tone that high-pitched,
insinuating wheedle Mother used when giving Simon orders.

Again, as he had done the week before, he stood back a
little.

'It's in the paper,' he repeated. 'Steve Biko died last week.
Last month he was taken. It's in the paper.'

My top lip was beginning to exude wetness. My hair burned.

'OK,' I said, retreating too. And then limply, 'Thanks.'

As he was again wiping his forehead, I missed seeing his
expression.

'Would you like some Oros and ice?' I asked, my voice, in
spite of myself, set bright and hopeful. But he was already
stooping as he shook his head.

Back in my bedroom, at my desk at the window, I could
watch him from the sheltered coolness, with a glass of cold
Oros, as I did every Saturday morning. The difference was
that the detachment had gone out of the scene. There was
the familiar bare back, sweat-contoured, at work; but now I
also had the memory of his voice. Again, I went over his words
in my mind. How should I take them? How to make sense of
what had happened? This was an odd kind of perplexity, a
feeling half of irritation and half of intrigue that I had no idea
how to manage. What was it, I asked myself, that Simon
knew? More than that, how had he come to know it? What
he had said was all news to me and that was strange. Was
Simon perhaps in touch somewhere with the dark black
underground of which Mother and the Reverend would speak
at the twilight-end of afternoons, in low tones as though
someone might overhear them? Somewhere there was a mys-
tery and perhaps even danger in all of this. I would have to
find out.

I did not spend much time that afternoon watching Simon.
As soon as Mother returned I set off for the town library.

The last year's newspapers were kept on open shelves in the small reading room at the back of the library, bound in plywood files. There was no one to disturb me here; the papers seemed not much read. But it was also tempting to nap dreamfully and often: the reading room seemed always to be close and warm, its two soggy armchairs warmer; the air conditioner, which emitted no coolness, had a soothing whir. Piling up the files at the end of the afternoon, I realised I might have to come back many times to find out what I needed.

The town of Merrydale is well placed on the landscape. Here, in a salubrious dell where a brown river runs and, rounding a bend, curdles to form a small white waterfall, large and comfortable bungalows lie scattered. These houses take up space and also require that much ground be spread between them. There is plenty of room to lay out flower gardens and swathes of lawn, courtyards of shredded stone, colonnades, rose arbours, wood-lattice gazebos. Cupped as though in a hand, wrinkled and wetted by the river tributaries, the verdant land thus proffers its beauties. The gesture, however, though generous, is not profligate. With the lawns so broad and the houses wide, the town stretches itself out expansively, reaching into farmland. But just as the botanical features in the gardens are balanced and matched – the spare rockery with the gay profusion of azaleas, the kikuyu grass lawn against the paved Japanese terrace – so too the town and the surrounding farmlands do not seem to exceed their boundaries, extending as far but no further than the horizon of enfolding hills. These were the hills that John Rudolph once embraced with a sweep of his arm and called his favourite view.

Only two main roads traverse this boundary: one goes to

the city, Hoopstad, an hour's drive away; the other leads in the opposite direction, off towards the steepest hills. This road branches out at an acute angle to the river, and narrows and grows circuitous as it negotiates the sides of the hills. Unlike the streets of Merrydale, this second road is not tarred. People live on the other side there, but what is puzzling is that no one in Merrydale goes over to visit, and at night the horizon shows no glow. Only in the clammy chill of an early morning, low smoke-cloud can be seen seeping over the hills and, some distance down the road, away from the town, rubbish is strewn all the way along the verges: plastic bags impaled on veld grass, beer cartons, old cardboard boxes and half-jack brandy bottles with the labels still bright. These are strange signs of life. They would make a first-time traveller here wonder. Most civilised people these days live cleanly, as they do in Merrydale, keeping nice the things that are theirs and the land that they own.

It is that time of year again, the *Merrydale Herald* said – and, by announcing the words, it was the time – the month of the final school examinations. Once again, our local reporter observed, the young matriculants shut their eyes to the summer sun, and set out to impress the examiners with all they know. In the streets of Merrydale, at the queues to the tills at the Superette, at the Wimpy bar where the rusty ice-cream machine whirred hot and loud, residents nodded at the young people they knew to be finalists. If, from local talent contests, or school magazine publicity, they recognised faces, they wished them well. Indeed, we all join in wishing them well, the newspaper said, adding that Merrydale was proud of its children. Heading the article on the front page was a group photograph of the local composite hero, the class of finalists so closely crowded together that it was difficult to piece out individual faces. A parent might simply place a hand over the picture and say, These are ours.

At the November meetings of the History Society, the talk during tea breaks was all of exams. One teatime, Mrs William Thomas, Chairwoman of the Society and wife of William Thomas of Klipspruit Farm, told Mrs Harmond, the Treasurer, in tones that carried, that she was proud of our youth. Her *Herald* was tucked under her arm. She said that children were the hope of a nation and its future. Some people, she knew, might feel uncertain about the time that lay before them – she was speaking discursively, pausing at intervals to sip tea – and, indeed, it had not been a very easy year in some ways for their beloved country. To the north, as they all knew, a sister nation was in distress. At times it might seem that the danger was very close. Last year of course they had had real trouble themselves – there was a general murmur of affirmative consternation – the black schools had been under attack; rabble-rousers had been on the rampage. But that was why our own children had to be encouraged – Mrs Thomas shifted her position that she might address the company more generally. When those others rejected all that had been given to them, she said, our children would continue to fulfil their duty to their society. That was why we could, and should, believe in them. Here Mrs Thomas began indulgently to dip her head to left and right, deferring to the nods and small sighs of her audience. Hear, hear, was Mrs Harmond's comment as she took Mrs William Thomas's empty cup.

Sylvie Rudolph had bought four extra copies of the *Herald* and cut out the photograph along its black framing edges. With Annemarie's face circled – far up in the corner, in the second row from the back – she sent off the cutting to her sisters and to Felix. Her own copy she kept on her coffee table, where she might look at it while knitting. It was a way of staying in touch. Sylvie was not only concerned about her daughter, as any mother might be, hoping Annemarie might bear up in the exams, but was missing her badly, which was also natural. During the past few weeks of this run-up to the exams, she saw Annemarie even less than before. Sylvie could hardly believe how little she saw her, seeing that they were mother and daughter and living beneath the same roof.

On the first Saturday in November, Annemarie, seemingly preparing for a siege situation in her mother's own home, had equipped herself with two generous armfuls of supplies: a ten-per-cent-extra pack of sanitary towels, an arm-and-leg stretcher-and-exerciser, her father's *History of the Years of Union*, an electric kettle, a woven grass fan with a green sprinkle motif – one of those that traditional blacks sell on the street – and also chewing gum, several packets, a catering can of instant coffee, and a de luxe vial of sweeteners. Now she probably thought she could avoid coming out of her bedroom even for short breaks. She had found a pair of her father's old khaki pants to wear, and she wore them till they smelt of yeasty crotch and that undefinable odour her sweat had – like tea gone cold and stale.

What made the sense of Annemarie's absence even worse was her spending afternoons away from home when, as far as Sylvie could see, it wasn't actually necessary. She said she needed to be in the town library. She explained she was revising: there was essential research that she had to do; the library was the only place for it. Also, yes, she was sorry, she might have to spend many hours there. But Sylvie couldn't help wondering if Annemarie was not deliberately trying to stay away. The worry worked at her, insistent as a child's fist.

Sylvie kept reminding herself that the situation remained more or less as the Reverend had diagnosed it – all part of acne and growing too fast and general truculence. But how could she get away from this fear that Annemarie was closed to her and that she, her mother, was forbidden access? Annemarie's room represented a blank, a kind of cordoned-off space in Sylvie's own home. If Annemarie was out, at school or in the library, Sylvie now entered it on tiptoe if she had to dust or to pick up dirty washing. The desk she was nervous to touch, even with the corner of the dust cloth; it seemed too precariously loaded. And then, when Annemarie was home, the door looked jammed, it was so firmly locked. Even when she came out on her occasional trips to the kitchen or the bathroom she left the door barely ajar – it seemed to stand ready to be closed again. Sylvie got nervous just thinking of it, of the stillness behind the door where her daughter was working.

Sylvie put more effort into trying to break this silence. One afternoon when Annemarie was at the library she slipped a glass bowl of alyssum sprigs from the garden on to the desk, in amongst the history books and papers. But Annemarie only scowled and said the things on her desk were not to be touched. The new lambswool comforter Sylvie made especially for Annemarie's room – all lacy loops and rose-pink, the colour Annemarie most liked when she was younger – met with a similar reception. Annemarie did not even shake it out to have a look when Sylvie gave it to her. She said thank you, she was grateful, but she didn't really have a need for such a thing at present. Folded exactly as it was, she put it in her cupboard.

After that Sylvie began temporarily to take the same dosage of tranquillisers as she had done at the time of John's death. It was to hold her peace; to have peace also. She and Annemarie might just as well have been tenants strange to one another, eating separate meals and leading separate lives beneath a shared roof space. Things almost felt better the times the girl was out of the house. When she was there in her room keeping to herself – well, the quietness defied one's powers of credulity.

Because of the child's continuing strangeness, Sylvie was hardly surprised when she discovered that Annemarie was not sleeping very well. Sleeping, after all, was a normal thing to do. Night after night, at four or five in the morning, Sylvie heard Annemarie stir, make coffee in her bedroom, make tea in the kitchen, pace in the living-room. Around by the sofa, Sylvie imagined her go, brushing along the length of the new curtains, across the carpet – the photographs and the tea set on the secretaire would be rattling – then round again by the sofa. After several nights of lying awake listening, Sylvie could stand it no longer: she had to go out to Annemarie – there was no help for it – she was already on her maximum dosage of Valium. Sylvie crept down the passage to check what Annemarie might be doing. She hoped she might be memorising her work, reciting facts, perhaps. But, as always, apart from her footfalls, the child was making no sound.

After nearly a fortnight of such goings-on, Sylvie decided to speak.

'Is there anything I can do?' she called through the closed door. 'Annemarie, little one, let me help.'

'I'm all right, Mother,' Annemarie called back. 'I'm sorry I woke you up.'

Sylvie went back to bed, but slept only with the dawn, when she heard that Annemarie had returned to bed.

More wakeful nights followed. Their eyes showed the strain. Sylvie felt that the veins in her eyeballs, red and swollen, were chafing against the lids. What was worrying the girl? she kept asking herself. It couldn't be the exams merely – that wasn't like Annemarie. Whatever was biting her was serious: she seemed to be even more preoccupied than usual. Sylvie suspected she might not be keeping her journal as diligently as she had before. Pretending to tidy Simon's work in the garden, Sylvie had watched Annemarie at her window. She could just see her staring out from between the parted curtains. Sylvie was sure Annemarie was not writing, or, anyway, not bent over her book in the old intent way. That was surely a bad sign too.

Could circumstances have brought her almost to the point of wishing Annemarie was writing? At one time, not even so long ago, Sylvie could not have believed it. But now she wished it – she prayed for it. Writing at least meant doing something. Writing she could conceive of as filling time. Night watches followed by daylong inanimation – this was beyond her. Even she, during that time of her bereavement, had not sat idle. It might have suited her to spend all day in bed. To dream and keen, refuse food and speech. But she had not done so. During her own adolescence, then too, Sylvie remembered, she had gone on more or less as normal. True, Christina used sometimes to have little moods, and would go off by herself to mope in the back garden. But they always managed to jog her out of that pretty soon. At home you had to look alert and bright, or else her father would have had something to say.

Around mid-November, just before the start of examinations, Sylvie began to check more closely what Annemarie was doing. There was no help for it. Was it not in Annemarie's interest also? Sylvie wanted to make sure she was studying. So if Annemarie was not in her room and her door stood a little ajar, Sylvie edged it slightly further open. Just to spot evidence of some kind of activity within. There were, Sylvie saw each time, enough books and newspapers about to suggest that the child was not completely neglecting her schoolwork. But, then again, she might still be dreaming over her books. Open files might not be proof enough.

One day, when Annemarie was in the living-room listening to the news on the radio, Sylvie ventured further in. She stumbled over a bathroom scale and a rubble of files on the way to the desk. The curtains damped out the light. On the desk, sheets of loose paper were thickly interleaved. Annemarie had been unearthing her history file. That seemed promising. Sylvie saw she was studying something like the modern history of the nation. She had put it down here: 'nationalism', 'self-determination', 'separate development' – key words in a list entitled 'Possible Important Questions'. She hadn't filled in anything more. Still, the endeavour looked like it was going somewhere. It could be, please God, that Annemarie was revising after all.

But Sylvie was thrown off balance once again by the ferocity of Annemarie's frown when, stepping out of the room, she encountered her daughter coming through into the passage from the kitchen. As they drew closer, they avoided each other's eyes. Sylvie saw only the fault line running down the middle of Annemarie's forehead. Annemarie was holding four thin slices of unbuttered white bread, two in each hand. When she reached Sylvie, she piled all four on one bony wrist in order to support herself against the wall with her free hand. Sylvie opened her mouth to explain, but Annemarie interrupted her. Annemarie reminded her mother that her room was her own space. What had she been doing there? Had her papers been moved?

'Annemarie,' Sylvie retorted, indignant, 'that's no way to speak to your mother; your father could have told you that. And anyhow, you know I sometimes go in to clean. Perhaps you don't realise how messy that room is. A mother sees these things. Cockroaches will come crawling out of it before long.'

Annemarie's scowl did not unclench.

'I need my private space,' she said. 'I need space to myself. I have to feel safe about that.'

'But, daughter of mine,' said Sylvie reasonably, 'perhaps if you were a little less alone, you'd feel less stressful. You're so nervous, so on edge.' She had to pause. Taking a breath, she found she could continue. 'Sometimes I don't recognise my little one in you any more. If you got out a bit, had a change of scene once or twice a day, wouldn't that feel better? You'd probably sleep more anyway.'

Transferring her bread to two hands again, Annemarie tried to get past her mother. Her eyes were fixed on the floor.

'I do get out,' she said, obdurate. 'I go to the library.'

Though she may once have discounted her words, Sylvie again phoned Mrs Lovemore. Not wanting to repeat old complaints, Sylvie spoke only of Annemarie's insomnia. This time, though, Mrs Lovemore seemed less forthcoming. Sylvie was perplexed. Seeing as she'd been managing to get out more and was surely striking a chattier note, couldn't Mrs Lovemore have been a little more responsive?

'Mrs Rudolph,' Mrs Lovemore finally began, 'Elise and Annemarie are not in close contact. Annemarie apparently told Elise one day at school that she wanted to study alone. She actually said quite openly she didn't need company. So there you go. What help could we possibly give?'

'Her aloneness is terrible, Mrs Lovemore,' said Sylvie. 'Recently she has started going to the library. She goes quite often. And I know she really does go. I called Mrs Sargeson, at the library, to confirm it. But while she's there she still keeps to herself, Mrs Sargeson told me. The change of scene changes nothing.'

'Well, I don't know, Mrs Rudolph,' said Mrs Lovemore. 'All I can say is talk to her again. The finalists are meeting regularly for tennis and cold drinks these days, to keep their spirits up, you know. If Annemarie tried to come along once or twice, I'm sure she'd feel a lot better. She must make the effort to help herself.'

Sylvie felt the cartilage of her ear beginning to take the strain of the mouthpiece.

'Yes, Mrs Lovemore,' she said.

'Anyway, I'm sure that things will improve once exams are over,' Mrs Lovemore went on, buoyed up by her own advice. 'Then you'll see something. The kids will be so happy. Then at least you and I can relax a bit. But not for long, I wouldn't think. I believe some of them are already organising the end-of-year party.'

Sylvie gave the requisite conspiratorial murmur, expressing a little reluctance and a large amount of relief. She agreed she could not wait for December.

But the nights of sleeplessness, Sylvie could feel, were placing her under strain. When, at five o'clock the following morning, she again heard Annemarie moving about, Sylvie went out to plead with her; to suggest hot baths and regular meals, or tennis and cold drinks, and more time with her mother. These things, any combination of them, might help. Sylvie brought her sleeping pills along with her. She pressed the phial into Annemarie's resistant fingers. She proposed Annemarie at least make an attempt to get things off her chest. Surely it wasn't only the present situation, the prospect of exams, that was bothering her? Surely it must be something more, something deeper, of the heart?

Annemarie did not deny it. She sat down as her mother spoke. Sylvie felt a little less diffident. If it was that Annemarie was thinking of upsetting things, she coaxed, please just to say it out loud. To unburden a heavy heart was a good thing. Could Annemarie not do this, if only in consideration towards her mother? Was it perhaps that she was beginning to think about someone at school in a special way – someone she would like to tell her mother about? Heartache, you know, happened to everyone at some time and was best shared. Or was it loneliness – not having a proper close friend to visit? Or could it be that Father's death was only now beginning to take its toll? Well, that too was only natural.

It was at this point that Annemarie gave a nod. Sylvie caught the movement. It was something to do with Father, then? Cupping Annemarie's chin in her hand, she brought the child's head up so that she could look into her eyes. Annemarie could not refuse the gaze. She said well, yes, perhaps Father did come into it. Perhaps, yes, she had been thinking about him. What then, what then? Sylvie asked. What is it you've been thinking? Tell your mother, Annemarie.

She'd been thinking, said Annemarie, pulling back, clasping her hands and shoving them between her legs, well, thinking back to the time before Father was ill, trying to remember things he had said, what he had said about what he believed – if Mother remembered? Like that time at Cantonville, the time with Uncle Felix – all those things Father had been saying, when he was explaining what he thought was right. He had been very angry, and also very straightforward. He had said, banging his hand on Aunt Elna's dresser, it was this way and no other. Did mother remember?

Here Sylvie saw a way in. She suddenly saw what had been going on in the child's mind. She knew what she had to say. Never doubt your father – Sylvie spoke the words hastily but firmly – never think ill of him. He was a good, upstanding man – surely that was clear? No matter what Annemarie might learn to the contrary, perhaps in those modern history books of hers, his beliefs were sound; there was a point to what he believed and he had stuck to it. For that, his constancy, his integrity, and also his reasonableness, he was an admirable man. Sylvie had said it before, she would say it again: one could only have regard for what he stood for; how he had faith in this country; how he had worked to make their lives good. Apart from that one difference they had regarding religion – which, though important, was redeemable – she still believed in what he had believed; she would always do so. Always believe in him. In all, she repeated, that he had believed. In all? said Annemarie. In all, said Sylvie. I stood behind your father in everything. Of course. Because he was right.

They stared at each other for some time, Annemarie vacantly, Sylvie with concern. Early bird-song began to rub at the night silence. They both stirred.

'I wanted to hear for sure,' was what Annemarie said next.

'There is nothing in what your father thought or did that should worry you,' said Sylvie.

As Annemarie turned away, Sylvie reached out for her. Putting her arm around her, Sylvie drew Annemarie's sharp shoulder against her breast.

If most of 1977 went by in a mood of abstraction, then the November of that year, which I simply do not remember as having passed, was, in a manner of speaking, erased from the calendar. At every point during that month I felt that I was elsewhere. I had by now stopped turning my days over into romance. I didn't feel much like writing at all. During the time I spent sitting at my desk, though my journal lay open before me, I stared off into the space ahead of me and into the hailscreen in front of it.

It was a peculiar time, a time of dismay. I rarely slept, rarely ate, and, on account of the diet pills, my heart seemed to revolve at speed in my rib cage. I was very thin. My hair, which had grown long, fell out in tufts when I brushed it. Mother's voice came to me from a distance, as though she spoke to me in sleep. From my window I watched her on the verandah with the Reverend; his hand was on her wrist. I hoped only that he might pacify her – for long enough anyway to give me time alone.

I was glad that he himself did not try to talk to me. The fact of exams helped. Exams effectively sealed me away. I saw no one and towards the end of the final term we were given time off from school. I told my classmates, the one or two I used to meet with to do homework – Elise Lovemore, Craig Brown – that I would probably not be seeing them very much over the next few weeks. I wanted to concentrate on my history, I told them, read widely, look at the archives at the library. Elise's gaze may have been curious but everyone got the message. No one called.

So the hours passed with a rapid merge effect, in an adrenalin stupor. I sat at my desk and did things with newspaper texts. I pasted clippings and photocopied articles into the back of my journal; I made summaries and tabulations – how much unrest in one month last year, how many deaths. I brought a roneoed map of the country home from school and coloured the trouble zones in black as I learned their names. But mainly I occupied myself with copying out the first paragraphs of newspaper reports verbatim. I soon had to switch to a new journal book – the last one was a concertina of clippings and glue-hardened pages and would not close. I tried to test myself on the information I was gathering – memorise names, events, dates. It may have been the diet pills, but I seemed to retain very little. Perhaps it was also, as I have said, that I did not know how to manage the new information – shape sentences to what I was discovering. Now that I had stopped composing my life for my journal, I had no way of connecting and so possessing the days which passed.

Sometimes, to make a change, to ease the dull ache in my

buttock bones, I went to stand in the middle of my room – to recite the facts there, and to try to think. Wherever I moved I seemed to stumble over and spill piles of school notes. These I had not looked at for weeks. The hours went by very quickly. I might begin an afternoon memorising information recorded on, say, a back page of my journal. I would mark off the facts as I memorised them, checking them mentally against the chicken wire hexagons of the right vertical side of my hailscreen. By nightfall I might have completed half such a column. I worried how I could ever begin to remember all that I had written down.

From my window I watched summer invade the garden. The plants seemed restless; they grew quickly. The trees, showing new leaves, reached perilously closer towards each other. I watched so long from my window that I was sure I saw the grass stretch. Simon was not there to mow it. He too was writing exams. It was that time of year again. Last year he had also been given the month off but had not written. The schools – that is, the township government schools – were empty; the students were in the streets. This the newspapers had told me. They were burning their own amenities was the comment. They throw their slop into the face that watches over them, said my history master – once – and then went back to the Reformation; they know not what they do, said the Reverend. But this year the subversive elements have been dealt with, said Mother, so Simon can safely write.

I thought of Simon somewhere in the school over the hill, in the town that I had never seen. I could not imagine how it would look. They cannot have new books and swimming pools like you children do, said Mother, the history teacher, everyone; conditions are simply not the same in their case; they are different, they cannot live as we do. But I was confused. From what I read I understood that people on both sides – the whites and the blacks – were upset; had in fact

76

been very upset. But that surely did not mean there was no help for it. The way I saw it, it meant only that something should be done. Conditions might be different, people might be angry; all this was possible. But help surely was possible too. Help neither offended nor hurt anyone. We – here on this side – should help them – on that side, over the hill – in some way. Like giving things, or collecting books, perhaps. We could go over on a fact-finding mission. Just generally to be of some use.

But my ideas for helping soon gave out. Yawning, I went off to write my exams. I thus became part of the substantial examination turnout throughout the country which was reported by the papers. The reporters sounded pleased. At the end of it all, I took four of Mother's sleeping pills – the ones she had given me herself – slept an entire weekend away and missed the finalists' celebration party.

Waking up on Sunday night, I was afraid I might also have missed Simon's return. Had he come on Saturday? I was eager to find out, but at the same time loath to ask Mother. I needed to speak to Simon again. I had to tell him I had done my reading. More than this, though, I had to tell him that I didn't know what to do with what I'd read. Which would naturally be a way of saying I wouldn't mind trying out ideas he might suggest.

I had to wait to hear these ideas. Simon did not appear until the weekend before Christmas, when he came to pick up his Christmas bonus.

Sylvie had decided where she would take Annemarie this Christmas; a place new and yet not entirely strange to them: the trip must be a treat and a break, but restful. She would take Annemarie down to the coast where her sister Elizabeth lived. They hadn't been to the sea or visited Elizabeth at home in several years. In her last letter Elizabeth had announced that their new place was at last spick and span and ready for guests. Some months ago she and her family had moved out of the congested bluff suburbs of town and had bought a place, a modest duplex, she said, situated in amongst respectable beach hotels. It had needed some alterations but was otherwise beautifully located; in the evenings it caught the sea breeze.

Sylvie felt full of end-of-year excitement. Her time was taken up with making plans. There was gift shopping to do: she must find presents for Annemarie and Elizabeth and Frank, and also for Elizabeth's two children. Mrs Roberts, the street neighbour with the azalea garden, whom she'd got to know better through the History Society, she asked to keep an eye on her property. The Reverend checked the electrical fittings in the house and, because Simon was still away, secured the hailscreens where the hooks or the netting had come loose. Sylvie, watching him work, told him he should think of finding a wife soon – his hands were the capable ones of a father. The Reverend looked away, bit his lip and said that thoughts of settling down had occurred to him too. Then he suggested that Sylvie think of putting in burglar-guards . You couldn't be too careful in these times – everyone knew that. Sylvie telephoned the police and asked them to keep a look-out while they were away. She made an appointment with a burglar-guarding company for January. She told the Reverend she felt safe enough. After all, only Simon could take word across the hills and he was probably to be trusted. Last year, of course, had been a troubled time for all blacks who were not rabble-rousers, but this year, thank God, there was less cause to worry. The children had gone back to school. The streets were once again quiet. Things were better. We can indeed thank God for that, the Reverend agreed.

Standing at the kitchen stable door, waiting as she counted out his *bonsela*, Simon told Sylvie that he had passed OK, A-1, no problem. Good, said Sylvie, good boy, adding a brown note to the pile for good measure. Merry, merry Christmas, madam, thank you, happy new year, said Simon.

Annemarie too had passed her finals, but not well enough to obtain an entrance to university. Sylvie had to admit she was surprised and yet at the same time not overly perturbed. The Reverend, of course, because he had their concerns at heart, shook his head and made comforting sounds when, the weekend before leaving for the coast, Sylvie told him the news. Sitting across the glass-topped cane table from him, Sylvie raised a pacifying hand in response. If Annemarie did not go to university, she explained, it meant she could stay longer at home. There was no reason, or none that Sylvie could see anyway, in young people leaving their families so early, only to go off to far, strange cities and in most cases run into trouble. What was the use of it? Instead, Annemarie might want to attend a secretarial course somewhere close to home. She should take time to think about her future. So Sylvie wrote away to the technical college in Hoopstad for application forms. She did not mind doing it for the child. You could understand that Annemarie herself did not yet want to make the effort. She needed rest. God might also be thanked that the child seemed to be sleeping again. The new year, Sylvie was sure, would bring better times.

I was at last able to intercept Simon the day he came to collect his Christmas bonus from my mother at the kitchen door. At the garden gate I waited for him. He came down the concrete path whistling noiselessly. He was wearing long khaki pants and a faded T-shirt that still spelt out, though vaguely, the name of the Bay City Rollers. His eyes carefully avoided spotting me.

'Simon,' I said prematurely, for he was not yet within close speaking distance, 'can I speak to you? I want to tell you something.'

He had stopped to listen. But the closeness of him made me less sure what to say.

'I went to read the newspapers. You know, the national news. Like you said I must.' The words came out uncertainly, each statement on an interrogative note.

He was standing listening, scuffing at the alyssum border with his foot. He said nothing. I had to continue.

'I read about Biko and all that,' I said. 'You know. The riots last year. And how people have been dying. But the papers don't say enough. I've been trying to find out things, but there's a lot more I think I need to know.'

Simon's reaction arrested my speech. He chuckled under his breath.

'Hey man, you were reading!' he said.

'Yes,' I started up again. 'I'd never read anything like it before. What's so incredible to me is that it was actually happening – '

Simon cut me off with a horizontal movement of an open hand.

'So,' he said, suddenly serious. 'So you've read the stuff. So what do you want to know now? You live here.' He gestured towards the house and quickly scanned its windows. 'We live there.' He was pointing with two hands. He brought his hands closer together, describing a space. 'This,' he said, jabbing his chin at the hand closest to him. 'This is our business.'

Biko, the papers had said, called for his people to stand together to find strength. He said they had to do it alone. It was the only way in which solidarity and pride could happen.

80

Is this what Simon was also saying? I should ask him. For my part, I couldn't see why more separateness was necessary. That's what Father wanted. But I wanted to help. To get rid of upsets you had surely to make peace – maybe to make friends. This must be possible.

'What I'm saying is not a hating thing.' I became aware of Simon speaking the words. 'What's important is for us to stand up for ourselves. We blacks. We must sort out our own freedom, our own lives. We don't need the whites for that.'

He stood awkwardly for a moment, as though there were more but he did not feel the inclination to say it.

'Look,' he finally said, 'you can meet me in town? Five this afternoon? For five minutes. At the – maybe – bus depot?'

I couldn't think of anything to say in reply. I felt suddenly intensely disappointed. For weeks I had waited for the advice Simon might be able to give. I wanted him to see that. Wasn't he aware of the effort I had put into finding out about things – the hours I had spent, the confusion I suffered?

'OK?' said Simon, already moving off, his mouth shaping back into a whistle. 'See you.'

The bus depot was located at the edge of town where the road broke the municipal boundaries to find its way around the hills to that neighbouring settlement of which no one spoke. It was a bare open space, untarred, gutted with mud pools and without shelters. In the shade of the eucalyptus trees on the one side, women whose gravid wealth of hip and breast seemed to graft them to the earth sold curried *vetkoek*, oranges, packets of snuff and green mealies displayed on chequered blankets. The iron-rank dust, stirred up by the turning and grinding of the buses, covered wares, passengers and eucalyptus trees like an infestation of minuscule red ticks.

During daylight hours the place was clamorous with movement. Labile busloads, expanding with a power of noise, brought workers into Merrydale: janitors, street sellers and sweepers, nannies, hairdressers' assistants, gardeners. When the dust settled red on the horizon of hills at night, these same were carted off again, the bus engines whining. At night the place was empty. The road across to the next valley was barred: no bus travelled it; no one came into town. The traveller on foot would do well to keep to the cover of darkness.

Next to the bus depot was the police station, a square brick bungalow in the style of a colonial railway building. The yard before the station was gravelled and fringed by an aloe hedge. The hedge masked the windows of the building. This was where I came with Mother to report our Christmas absence. The offices had been very warm, the flushed constable sleepy. Most police activity happened out at the back, Mother explained, her tone reassuring. At the back was a guarded entrance where police vehicles would drive out suddenly in a maelstrom of dust and return bearing passengers.

It was because of the visit with Mother that the bus depot was not entirely strange to me. Before then, I had not come near it. I had never had to use the buses: they were black buses, so using them was unthinkable. I knew of the existence of the place: I might be able to point it out to a stranger. I knew the dust there was terrible. But the place was too far out on the edge of town – too black, it was said – for a girl like me to go out there alone. So when at four that day I prepared to leave, I did not tell Mother where I was going. To forestall questions, I took my library books with me. I was glad of these books when, standing in the shade of the eucalyptus trees, I waited for Simon. By holding them in front of me, against my chest, I would be showing the curious that I had an errand to run.

At five minutes to five Simon found me. He came up from the side of the parking bays, along the lines of the bus queues, so I did not at first see him. He squatted beside where I was standing. I started. I had backed around the side of the clump of trees, out of sight of the crowd.

'Hello,' he said, without looking at me. It took me by surprise to see how much at ease he was compared to our interviews back at the house. His hands were drooped loosely on his knees; his eyes rested on concentrations of activity in the five o'clock crowd, but without particular interest, like one who enjoys a well-known spectacle. A man was selling groundnuts from a vendor's tray without handles. Simon hailed him and they exchanged sentences. I did not understand what they were saying.

Their conversation attracted the attention of one of the women selling fruit near by. She and Simon engaged in a series of questions, after which she energetically got up, shook out her blanket, and spread it again, making sure that the corners were well straightened out.

'She is showing you can sit down there,' said Simon.

'She shouldn't have gone to the trouble.'

'She wants it. She is an old mama. That makes her happy.'

I went over and sat down. Again, Simon squatted beside me.

'You want a Coke?' he asked.

I reached for the purse in my pocket.

'No,' he said emphatically but without volume. 'I got my Christmas bonus, jy weet. I will get it.'

At this comment he may have tried to catch my eye – his tone suggested this could be a kind of joke, such as on the day Mother called from the verandah. But I was unsure where to look or how exactly to compose my lips, so I kept my chin down and sat on my hands. I wished the woman whose blanket I was sharing would not stare at me so fixedly. While Simon was away I slightly turned my shoulders away from her.

He returned with one bottle of Coke only, which was already half empty. My gut recoiled. Simon seemed to have overestimated my enthusiasm for our encounter – or otherwise he was testing me. Which would explain why he was openly watching me drink. And why, when I finished, his eyes did not leave my face. He was, I felt sure, checking to see whether I would wipe my mouth.

'Mm hm,' he said.

I felt oddly exposed. The shapes of old phrases used by people like my father for political parry and attack crowded into my throat but remained stuck there. I thought of Simon's mug at home, washed separately by Mother.

We both stared out at the crowd. I wanted to ask him about the purpose of my coming. What exactly was his plan? What was he thinking to offer me? I made up several questions in my mind, yet each opening seemed either too chary or too avid. I began to think of the time.

'You came here before?' he said at length, without changing his position.

I shook my head but as he was looking ahead he could not have seen the motion clearly.

'If you did not come here before, you would not see this place is busy today. Bu-sy.' He drew out the two syllables. 'Everybody has got their bonselas from the bosses and the madams. Now they will spend money in the white shops. Today people are happy.'

'I can see that.' I tried to speak on a rising tone – with encouragement, helpfully. Being helpful had been, after all, my original intention.

'You want to know things? Now I'm showing you,' he stated.

His manner was decisive. Had he perhaps interpreted my ingratiating tones as condescension? I moved round slightly in order to face him.

'You don't know these people,' he went on, his voice lower. 'Do you know our language? Do you know where we live?' He did not pause for a reply. 'No. You know nothing. What is the work of these people? Where do they work? Do they like the work? What do they want really? Do you know? No.'

The negative was a statement, but even so I shook my head and repeated, 'No.'

'Then we must sort out our shit,' he said. 'You guys have given us the shit. But we can sort it out. We will sort it out – alone. We can do it.'

We were now looking at each other full in the face.

'What are you saying? That it's all separate anyway? That I don't have a place here – I must go?'

'You want me to tell you what to do?' Simon asked quizzically. And, as an afterthought, with what seemed an arch smile, 'Like you maybe also want me to tell you, Thank you, madam, for coming? Please, madam, come again?'

The wish to go home was strong in me. By now several people were watching us: the woman, a neighbour of hers, the groundnut vendor, two young boys who looked like touts. I wondered whether the police could also have sighted our meeting. Simon may have had the same thought. He moved off a little, swivelling on his haunches. I wanted to ask, Can I go now? I thought of saying, Thank you. I said neither. I tried nodding to the woman who had spread the blanket, but she had turned towards her companion. I got up.

'Ja. See you. Thanks for coming,' Simon said.

I screened my eyes against the light of the low sun, trying to scan his face for a twinge of sarcasm. I was too slow; Simon was already moving off. I dusted my legs. To get out to the main road, I had to pass the groundnut vendor. I gave him five cents. He poured a large handful of swollen nuts into my spread palms. A number spilled out. 'Thank you,' I said, and did not look up.

That summer, at the beach resort on the Cape coast where Elizabeth lived, the states of matter seemed to exist in transition. The tar sweated; window frames suppurated resin. The sea, dispersing itself as vapour, was everywhere – inside the cupboards and beds, on food and skin. Petrol stations wavered in heat hazes; roads and bright beaches dissolved into radiant light.

Sylvie and Elizabeth were most often found sitting in the shade of the avocado tree in the garden patch. The strip of duplex garden, inserted between two beach hotels for pensioners, was quiet and private and, because of the avocado tree, cool. Sylvie and Elizabeth immersed their feet in bowls of tepid water, which they refreshed at intervals with ice. In their hands they held cotton crochet work of filigree delicacy but without form. Crocheting had been their mother's favourite kind of handwork. They might have been following one of her old patterns, they might have been making something Sylvie had found specially for the occasion in a magazine. But as their hands were often still to give opportunity to the celerity of their tongues, there was no way of telling. Sylvie and Elizabeth felt that between them they had about five years' worth of news to share. They agreed that letters gave no more than rudimentary impressions of events, and that family gatherings – of which there had been sadly few of late – did not allow sisters to sit down for good long chats over tea. A great deal of their news had to be reviewed and retold. To help them pass the hours of conversation more comfortably, Sylvie and Elizabeth enlisted the services of Frank, Elizabeth's husband. Frank had bad circulation, kept his own counsel and was himself a pensioner. He helped by making tea and fetching ice, and, where necessary, supplied corroborative murmurs.

As evening fell, and the sea breeze began to blow, Sylvie and Elizabeth retreated into the kitchen to spend hours over summer recipes in thirty or more steps, delicacies their mother had made without effort and in no time. As they prepared the food, and washed each piece of cutlery as they used it, they remembered their mother, and spoke well of her.

Of their children, Annemarie, and Peter and Paul, her cousins – but especially of Annemarie – they spoke in practical terms during the day and more intimately at night. In the kitchen Sylvie, dropping her voice, explained how much Annemarie had worried her – the child had been half sick, not eating, not sleeping, not ever getting out into the open air. She now hoped, however, that matters were on the mend. Just between the three of them, it was her opinion that this holiday could – touch wood and God willing – work wonders. Her cousins' company, the sea air, leaving her books behind – yes, Sylvie had to insist on that – all these things would do Annemarie a power of good.

In the kitchen at night Sylvie spoke also of John, of how she still missed him. Frank, peeling potatoes, made his comforting velar sounds as he listened. Over and over Sylvie stressed that nothing, not her church involvement, nor her very valuable relationship with the Reverend Guthrie – what a fine man he was – had quite filled in the waste spaces of her life. Once again, though, she had hopes – hopes which were fastened on Annemarie.

Sylvie was chopping parsley for the soup the night she most emphatically expressed her hopes. She raised her chopping knife and fork and held them like batons as she spoke. Despite the difficulties of the last year and a half, she told Elizabeth and Frank, she had hopes that Annemarie would become more of a daughter to her. If Annemarie took the next year easy – as indeed she should, if she knew what was good for her – then they might be able to spend more time together. They could get to know each other again. How happy that would be. She should add, though – Sylvie knocked the knife blade against the fork – that staying at home need not tie Annemarie down. There were all sorts of things Annemarie might like to, and could, in fact, do. There were lots of interesting groups on offer in Merrydale, like the History Society, for example. Sylvie herself had met people through the Society, and then too, history was Annemarie's abiding interest.

Elizabeth's reply was a little unexpected. She asked if Annemarie had ever had a boyfriend. Sylvie crossed the fork and the knife on the board and scraped up the parsley she had been chopping in her hands. Shaking the moisture out of the parsley, Sylvie said Annemarie's interests did not run that way – Annemarie was more of a homebody. It was Sylvie's feeling that young people started those things too young anyway. There are so many better things to do with time, was her private thought, than to fester together in bedrooms.

'But isn't there a certain value in boys getting to know girls?' Elizabeth asked.

'There's plenty of time for that,' said Sylvie, still squeezing the parsley. 'Annemarie is very young. She's hardly developed. Have you seen her hips? And she has less breast on her than other girls her age, less, in fact, than when she was younger, when at least she had some flesh.'

'Times may have changed,' said Elizabeth.

Sylvie smiled in a blank way that indicated she might like to terminate the conversation.

'These new ideas are all very well,' she said. 'But one can never be too careful.'

Going over to the stove, scattering her parsley, stirring the soup with a firm stiff wrist, Sylvie expressed her conviction that their generation, hers and Elizabeth's – this with a little smile for Frank – had surely been happier innocent. If it lay within her power she would help Annemarie in staying innocent. The Reverend Guthrie, whose opinion she would not quickly begin to doubt, was entirely in agreement with her. And Annemarie did not seem to be resisting. Also, one should not forget that Elizabeth came to the thing from a very different perspective: she had sons. Elizabeth acknowledged that Sylvie had a point there: yes, she said, she had to admit sons were far less worry. Frank nodded his agreement.

Annemarie spent that summer holiday in the company of her cousins Peter and Paul, but especially of Peter, who was older and had a cleft chin. For much of the time they lay on Peter's bedroom floor listening to Pink Floyd and staring at the ceiling. To go to the beach in the heat required considerable effort. At night they drifted down to the building lot at the end of the street, where more hotels were to be built, so Peter could smoke the skinny joints he scored off the ice-cream man.

Because of her mother waiting back at the house, Annemarie smoked only once – one cool late evening. The sky that night was luminous; the dispersed heat hazes of the day reflected back the lights of the esplanade. They had leaned their bare shoulders against one another, she and Peter, and he had pressed her free hand in his. They had told each other repeatedly, during the joint and after, that things were good.

Things were so good that Annemarie began slowly to feel she had been absolved of memory and of effort. Her synapses were carelessly fraying and there was nothing she need ever do about it. She breathed in deeply and out again and heard her lungs sigh their satisfaction. She perceived all of a sudden that things need not be as difficult as she had imagined. She had cherished impossible, romantic ideas, she now realised, ideas gratifying to contemplate: she had wanted to make forbidden friends, do great, good deeds – but perhaps her life could not take the mould of these ideas. Courage and sacrifice – or whatever it was that might be required, she did not know – these might be beyond her. Fictions were anyway difficult enough on paper. She should have seen much earlier that events couldn't be worked in the same way as words. Simon had at least, though indirectly, pointed to her folly; she could thank him for that. Simon had shown that what happened in the world resisted remaking. Wanting to help didn't work. She had to accept this fact.

Annemarie shrugged and Peter adjusted the position of his shoulders. She noticed that the stone beneath her hand was warm and sleek to the touch. She let her legs go slack. At the same moment it occurred to her that there might be little point in making an effort and doing anything at all. Or not for the present, anyway, not while it was so pleasant to feel the closeness of the earth and a cousin's firm back, and, touching her face, the cool breath of the land wind moving out to sea. This was an important perception, Annemarie realised, she must remember it well – maybe write it down. In these surroundings you saw everything quite clearly: you saw that it was good and right to think impossible things, to remember ambitious ideals, but only so long as you put no hope into them. Avoiding the stress of hope gave so much freedom to your thoughts.

*   *   *

One day, towards the end of the holiday, when they were drying out after a late afternoon swim, hunched up in their towels, Annemarie and Peter both felt suddenly and inexplicably disgruntled.

'I did not see the ice-cream man today,' Peter said.

'So, in that case, what shall we do tonight?' asked Annemarie.

'Paul has heard of a beach party.'

'I don't feel like a party.'

'Nor me.'

'So let's do something different.'

'I'll dare you then.'

'Dare.'

'We could do it.'

'You read my mind.'

They visited the late-night chemist, giggled at the choice of condoms displayed on the personal health and hygiene shelf, and fumbled at the counter with coins, for neither of the two had quite enough money. They might have made it to the building lot, had it been closer, but as it was they chose the parking space behind the Intimate Movie Theatre, where the cars were packed in tight for the early evening show. Negotiating the tricky leverage of a Volkswagen Beetle runningboard, they lost their shyness. Annemarie was briefly surprised that she felt neither the pain nor the humiliation for which her mother's darkly implied aversions had long prepared her. Peter at least cried out at the critical moment whereas she had to concentrate on keeping her head from knocking against the wing mirror. What was vaguely unpleasant, she thought, as she pulled her underwear back on, was having her nose squelched into the sweat on his chest. But otherwise, she decided, wiping her face and her thighs with the hem of her dress, she was glad the thing was over and done with. She opined the same to Peter, who agreed.

Annemarie recorded the event in her journal: a one-line sentence, stating the fact. It was the first regular journal entry she had made since November.

It is Christmas time. The cicadas are screaming as they always do at this time of year. As the heat rises the scream intensifies until it is a presence so continuous and fierce it is more than sound – it incises the ear.

The house, which on the best of days seems empty, has temporarily been left vacant. It lies flat and simple as a lost brick. Though the light is harsh without, it is dark within. The curtains are drawn; the screens are up. In a house where the human witnesses have left, it has been shown, rhythm of light suggests time passing. In this house, however, most light is excluded. Only dust falls: a greyness from within as the curtains sag, as newspapers, stuffed into a pile beneath a bed, compress, as the draught stirs; a red dust from without, brought in with the wind, from where the pasture ruptures. Dust fall is an unceasing accretion, without measured movement, unlike light.

Only at night there is a light, a slim feeler of torch-beam at ten, that traces the lineaments of the house, the rooftree that holds old carpets and antimacassars, the windows covered inside and out. The torchlight, held by the flushed hand of the man in uniform, needles along the chinks that the draught finds, cuts curtain slits, burns brief lacklustre suns on new linen.

But only once, and then during the day, does the man who might be called an intruder come. He has come to see to the flowers but the central bed is scorched, pressed to a silver medallion. Sleepy, he sits on the handle of a dry watering can, stretching his legs in the heat, facing the beauty of the view. His hand twists at kikuyu grass runners. When he leaves there is a single burst of noise. In the post-box at the gate he has dropped a large envelope: it holds an old newspaper; it is for Annemarie. Beneath the front door he has also slipped a note. It is for Mrs Rudolph. This will be his last visit.

The house stands. The dust falls. Inside and outside, time seems suspended, arrested by heat.

In mid-January the Rudolphs returned to Tintagel; by April they had moved out and left town. From the moment of homecoming, for her who had the eyes for it, the portents of disaster were plain to see.

The first thing Sylvie descried on getting home was the death among the flowers. Fear snatched at her breast. She ran towards the front door. The second thing Sylvie found was the note from Simon slipped under the door. Simon said he was very sorry but he had to leave. Sylvie gasped for the sake of her flowers. She murmured, 'Father.' But it was the third sign that brought forth her lamentation. The third thing that Sylvie discovered on returning home was the red dust that had dispersed itself throughout her house, the iron-rank dust that covered the piano ivories, the new linen upholstery, the bedclothes and the garments folded in the cupboards – spread thick on every surface like an infestation of red ticks.

Calling to Annemarie to stay within reach, Sylvie called the Reverend. The Reverend's maid said the master was still away. So Sylvie called Elizabeth. She told Elizabeth that they had arrived safely but disaster had struck: the house was invaded, the boy had absconded, the flowers were all dead. Annemarie, standing close, held by the wrist, asked if she might speak to Peter.

'No, certainly not,' whispered Sylvie. 'It's too far. It's too expensive. You've just seen him for three weeks.'

Elizabeth cried, 'What did you say?'

Sylvie called back, 'Nothing.'

They removed the dust by a process of slow blowing and brushing, Annemarie with the soft brush following Sylvie with the hard. Thereafter there was still unpacking to do and the police to thank for watching the house. It was only at supper, so preoccupied had she been before, that Sylvie remembered to ask Annemarie what manner of parcel she had received in the mail.

Annemarie said she was sorry but she could not say. Sylvie expressed amazement.

'You haven't opened it?' she asked.

'I have, but I can't say,' said Annemarie.

'You can't tell your mother what was in the parcel?'

'Mother, it's really not as important as it may look, but I'd still rather not say.'

Sylvie's heart fell heavily against the ladder of her ribs. If there was a sign bearing more foreboding than the dust, this must be it.

The mysterious parcel brought mysterious movements. Was it that Annemarie had sat silent and quiet before, and now cast about her bedroom, moving things around, that there seemed to be a rumour in the wind? Try how she might, Sylvie could not quell her unease. She prayed. But what she had once requested had been granted her: Annemarie had started to keep her mother company. Annemarie now offered to make dinner, filled in the forms for the secretarial college, sat on the verandah drinking tea. In late January, during a severe storm, she crouched with Sylvie under the dining-room table, gripped her hand, gave her gum to chew. When it was over, and the earth exuded pungency, she offered to replant Sylvie's flowerbeds. The seeds sprouted in a week.

Sylvie needed to speak to someone. She wished the Reverend was here. She longed for the touch of a restful hand. There was no rest in Annemarie, neither when she was tidying her bedroom, nor when she was mulling compost in the garden. Was it that the change in the girl had come too suddenly? Hither and thither, tirelessly, Sylvie now heard her stir – up and down the passage, around in the kitchen. Overnight she seemed to take up more space. Her smell, which had always been pungent, lay thick upon the air; Sylvie could not escape it.

'Do you still keep your journal as much as you used to?' she asked Annemarie.

It was a hot evening in early February. They were sitting in darkness, to forestall insects swarming in through the open windows.

'No, not as much,' said Annemarie.

'Why? Why do you write less?'

'Maybe because there is less to say.'

'You mean you're bored?'

'No, Mother, maybe I'm simply changing a little.'

Again, Sylvie's heart bumped against her ribs. The portents of danger, she could see, were everywhere. On Annemarie's top lip a blue haze grew. On Sylvie's back, a mole sprung into a corona, and required excision. Annemarie discovered white ants in the house foundations. In the dead of night their gnawing was like the tearing of multiple silk veils. Beneath the piano the floorboards rang hollow. There is an evil in my life I cannot name, Sylvie thought.

From the coast Annemarie received twenty premature Valentines in twenty red envelopes. At the same time she received another parcel: sender not given, postmark unclear. Again, she would not say what was in the parcel. The Valentines and also the parcel made her blush.

'Annemarie, do you like your mother?' asked Sylvie on another hot evening. 'Not necessarily love her, but like her?'

'We live together, Mother, don't we, without too much effort? We get on. We may not agree at all times, but that must be natural.'

'We don't agree?'

'Not always. I don't always agree with what you believe, for example.'

'With what I believe? What do you mean? Explain to me what you mean, so that we can sort it out and make things better. You do trust your mother, don't you, small Annemarie?'

'Yes, Mother, yes. It's just that there are some things we must sort out alone. I mean, there are things I must sort out alone – you know, for myself.'

Sylvie sensed perplexity. She could not, after all, be sure Annemarie was at rest so she, Sylvie, could not rest easy. Sylvie rearranged her room, removing the extra bed, John's bed. She renewed her subscription to the History Society. The burglar-guarding was installed. Annemarie too had rearranged her room – twice. The second time she removed most of the furniture except for the bed. She stored the extra furniture in the attic space together with the antimacassars. She took down her hailscreen and she refused burglar-guarding. She also refused membership of the History Society. Sylvie found she lacked the words to pray.

Part of the trouble, Sylvie reasoned to herself, might lie in the present quietness of the town. In early February things still seemed to be in recess, were somnolent with the heat. Societies were not yet meeting; the church was half empty; the Reverend was still away. It will all be better when term starts in March, and you begin commuting, Sylvie assured Annemarie.

'Mother, I'm all right,' said Annemarie.

'You sure you're not bored?'

'I've told you I'm not.'

'But perhaps you're lonely.'

'Mother, I'm writing to Peter. I've written away for back copies of newspapers. I plan to make up for what I missed last year. I like to be outside in the garden. I have a lot to do.'

Annemarie was putting in a new border of red hot pokers and agapanthus to run down one side of the garden, the side which faced the road and led off at right angles to the row of casuarinas. The job demanded digging and hauling, so on the hour Sylvie brought Oros and ice.

'I can hire a new boy, Annemarie,' she repeatedly said.

'This does me good.'

'On the contrary, I don't think any good can come of it. It just doesn't pay to push self-will quite so far. Work like this is not for bodies like ours.'

'I want to feel what it's like.'

Sylvie kicked a bulb, tumescent as a goitre.

'If you need work there's plenty of help you can give me indoors,' she said.

From the windows of the house as she dusted or knitted, Sylvie watched Annemarie in the garden. What could it be that was driving the girl now? She was almost as reticent as before, though more bluff. More than ever she sat with her scratched legs open. Sylvie wondered if the acquaintance with her cousins had been as beneficial as they had anticipated. It was since the vacation that the unrest which rummaged at her own breast had seemed to start working at Annemarie's limbs also. Since then, too, had come the parcels without name and the signs without cause. Sylvie was frightened. The photograph of her parental family – her father on the stoep of her maiden home, his wife and daughters around him – fell from the dining-room dresser, its frame and glass cracked across. Bruises like hydrangeas flowered on Annemarie's limbs, yet she complained of no pain. The centre stone disappeared from Sylvie's amethyst cluster brooch, her last gift from John. The day the stone fell out, Sylvie called the Reverend, long distance, to pray with him.

It occurred to Sylvie that, for all her protestations of innocence, Annemarie might, after all, be hiding a clue to her present mysteriousness in her bushels of papers. Her journals held information: why else did she guard them so well? What was known to one could well mean resolution for another. In Annemarie's scribbled writings must lie an index to what should be revealed.

Sylvie was sure that what she would discover could help them both. She was sure because when she walked into Annemarie's room that day with the intention of dusting, she found a prayer singing itself in her head. Because a prayer was in her head, Sylvie had new hope: she knew her perplexity could be resolved.

At first she was taken aback at the tidiness of the room. The floor was clear of papers, the books were on the shelves. Though the curtains were still half closed, the room seemed full of light because the hailscreen had been removed. Sylvie walked to the desk; she checked to left and right out the window. She saw Annemarie stretched across her hedge of red hot pokers; she realised Annemarie would give her time.

There was no need to fear discouragement: the journal was snibbed in amongst a pile of old hardbacked library books stacked on the floor beside the bed. Sylvie recognised its covers. Annemarie still used the exercise books John had held in storage for his accounts.

As she took up the familiar book, unease again leapt in Sylvie's breast. She was aware of a heat in her cheeks. After all, what she had seen once before in the journal – that strange column of statements – had driven her to appeal to the Reverend for help. Sylvie decided she would look only for a moment. The book fell open easily at the point where the writing ended. She saw that the lines, especially the last, were as curt as before, and the close lettering as difficult to decipher. She closed the book again, with her finger at the place, to adjust her focus. An eye muscle trembled.

Once more Sylvie checked that Annemarie was still working. It was possible to persevere. The script still defied her. She paged back one, two pages. Everywhere she noticed the epigrammatic insertions that hyphenated more florid passages. These shorter bits helped, marking off paragraphs, and so accustomed her to reading. Though she had to blush again and again, repeatedly, as she read, she did not give up.

Sylvie came back to the book after lunch. The meal had been difficult. Though Annemarie had scanned her face, possibly querying her silence, Sylvie did not look up. While the journal was in her mind's eye, she did not want to talk to Annemarie.

For the second reading, Sylvie had to take a seat on Annemarie's bed. Again she checked that Annemarie was in the garden, within sight. Once or twice Sylvie was sure she caught Annemarie staring directly at the bedroom window, but even had she laid down her spade and hoe and prepared to come in, Sylvie could not have put down her reading. What

Sylvie was discovering demanded to be read. Each sentence she unpeeled from the page revealed more that lay beneath. She hastened backwards and forwards across the text, cramming down pages with two hands. Truth was manifesting itself as rapidly as she could keep up with reading. When Sylvie looked up to make sure of Annemarie's whereabouts or to rest her eyes, runic images flared upon the walls and sky. Her retinas were inflamed by words.

Annemarie came in from the garden at dusk, sticky with sweat and plant juice. Sylvie was sitting watching television in the living-room, her knitting in her lap. The light of the setting sun in the golden room coloured her form in rose. Stripping off her T-shirt as she went, Annemarie called out that she was off to have a bath and find some coolness. From the door of her bedroom, as the T-shirt dropped from her hand, Annemarie saw the mark her mother had left behind her on the bed, the pressed fold marked by her buttocks. Quickly Annemarie went over to search the desk, to see if she had left newspaper clippings or letters – or worse, even, some sign of Simon's last missive – lying about. She checked the pile of books by the bed. The journal was in its place. She set off down the passage to the living-room. Her mother met her half-way there, at the passage door. Preparing to express the force of her indignation, Annemarie did not at first sight her mother's eyes.

'Mother, you've been in my room,' said Annemarie.

'I've been in your room?' asked Sylvie.

'Why do you do it? What do you want to know?'

'As your mother, I have the right,' said Sylvie a little unsteadily.

'What did you say?'

'I have seen things.'

'What is it you want to see? What is it I must tell you?'

'When things are hidden from her own mother by a daughter, the mother must somehow find out the truth.'

'Mother, I'm afraid I can't completely agree with you. I thought we both understood that I need room where I can be alone and private. Else I would have to start hiding things.'

'You have been hiding things,' said Sylvie, her eyes wide as though in surprise.

'I must be a person in my own right, Mother. With my own ideas.'

'You are a person,' said Sylvie, very quietly now, 'I do not know.'

The quietness of her voice gave no warning of the energy in Sylvie's next movements. As she finished speaking, Sylvie grabbed Annemarie by the shoulders so forcefully that they both winced. As suddenly she pushed her away. Then she grasped her again. She quickly pressed her forehead to Annemarie's crown; she crammed Annemarie's head against her shoulder. The heat of her mother's sorrow cooked Annemarie's flesh.

'My daughter,' said Sylvie, 'who are you? You are a person the like of which I could never have imagined. I have no idea who you actually are.'

As after my father's death, stating difficult things in simple terms is a way of bringing them to order.

Sometime during the first months of that hot new year, my mother took note of salient facts in my journal. The more descriptive fictive passages were not her concern. She was done with fictions. She had opened the book hoping to be reassured. She discovered everything that was dreadful to contemplate. Weeks afterwards she could recite word-for-word, pause-for-comma, in time with the to-and-fro rocking of her body, the sentences that spelt out a new and unimagined reality. One: that her daughter was a maiden no longer. Two: that the body that had rent my body was of our blood. Three: that though thus spoiled I had felt neither pain nor guilt. Four: that I had considered more of the same and with others. And, Five – or part of Four: that I had desired a man old enough to be my father.

She did not find out anything of my dealings with Simon. The November material was set in denser paragraphs – all the journalists' reports I had spent the long sedentary weeks of the exam period copying. Because of copying the reports, or of feeling preoccupied, I had neglected to write up some of the important times: like the afternoon of the confused disappointment at the bus depot, or – more recently – the equally confused gratification of the day we returned from vacation, when I found Simon had returned the borrowed newspaper with the message that I should hold on to it for safekeeping. As a follow-up to this had come the second parcel – it must surely be from Simon. Wrapped in the classified pages of a newspaper, advertisements for old stoves and masseurs, the parcel held an anonymous flyer: pale-green paper, blotched lithographic picture – the subject undetectable – and a quotation from someone called Frank Talk. This event, too, I had failed to record. I did not know what Simon had meant by sending the parcel nor how exactly to interpret the flyer. What could I report other than that this missive had arrived?

But these were obscure details for which Mother, at that time at least, had no interest. What she had hoped to find was hard proof of our bondedness. What she found instead was that the flesh of her flesh had, without her knowledge, obtained carnal knowledge. The word was not spoken but the feeling was betrayal. I had grown alien to her. For a time she withdrew hastily even from my inadvertent touch.

Days of a sort of unspecific, low-intensity discomfort followed. There were long periods of silence and long periods of repeated sighing during which I sat looking out of the window and Mother sat looking at me. Very little happened. There were some telephone calls: to her doctor, to Elizabeth, to the Reverend in his home town. The Reverend promised he would soon return; I was not permitted to speak to Peter. I heard that Elizabeth, too, and Frank, were in pain. There were pills, for Mother, for her pain. The first night, Mother had needed a new stock of tranquillisers from the emergency chemist. But, though she took these and others regularly and at frequent intervals, she still kept her arms closely clamped to her breast, as if to quieten her breathing.

To pacify her breathing, as we waited for the Reverend to return, we kept ourselves busy with stories. I was the narrator, first person personal; Mother checked the facts against her memory. She screwed up her eyes, the better to concentrate or to suppress what she could not bear to hear. Questions were reiterated and episodes retold. I spoke at some length; I could not refuse her. Though I had spent much time composing my own stories, I had not invented contingency plots – I did not have a set of more benign tales in stock. During the many months I had spent filling my journal days with words, I had not imagined this could ever really happen, this sudden concussion of her fictions and mine.

The Reverend Guthrie brought relief. Within an hour of his eventual coming, he and Mother retired to the seclusion of her bedroom to pray. I heard her voice rising, falling and rising. I heard them pray together, prayer after prayer. I feared they might at some stage call me in to join them, so I went walking. There was an errand I had to run for which I had not yet had the time. I walked to the edge of town, a place not far from the bus depot, the site of the municipal dumping grounds. It was a wide piece of land, covered with slowly smoking ash and hidden from the road by dense bramble bushes. It smelt distinctively of rust and pus. I did not spend very long. As soon as I arrived, I felt I had to hurry home. I was right in doing so. At the gate Mother was waiting: she wanted me to be with her during the Reverend's closing prayer. She said it would help her. I walked with her to the bedroom, she behind me. She asked where I'd been. I said to town and back – for air. That was, I think, the first lie I consciously told my mother.

At the suggestion of the Reverend Guthrie, the Rudolphs left Merrydale. Any anticipated upset of moving, they all agreed, would be counteracted by their more pressing distress. The walls of the house were now marked by insomniac transfixions; the lawn and flowerbeds, dry and untended, offended Sylvie's gaze. Along one side of the garden, a kind of red hot poker border still faltered: the bright pinnacles, imperfectly trans- planted, poked out at rakish angles; at its far end, the line dwindled to a prickle of shallow holes.

When Annemarie had told the tales she had to tell, the Rudolphs' conversation ended. They sat on the verandah drinking tea, Sylvie with her back to the yard and the view. From time to time, counting the stitches in her knitting, Sylvie observed it would take a while to get used to the new state of things. Annemarie did not reply. She was content now to spend the hours in silence, stretched out in her chair and staring at the hills. As she no longer wrote her journal nor read very much, she had the time. Through the medium of the Reverend, Sylvie again asked her why she no longer wrote.

Annemarie told him it was probably because she needed a break.

Since his return, the Reverend came round almost every day. If they were out on the verandah, he would, towards the end of a visit, come to stand between Sylvie and Annemarie, a hand placed on the shoulder of each. He would call them his sisters. He would say it was important to keep faith.

In the small city called Hoopstad, thirty miles from Merrydale, the place where Annemarie had been enrolled to attend the technical college, the Reverend found them a new home. What he chose, after to-and-fro telephoning with Sylvie, was a flat in a respectable flat building, four storeys high and five flats long. Their flat, the Reverend said, was on the top floor and faced south, away from the horizons where the storms emerged. They could dispense with hailscreens as well as with burglar-guarding. Their flat block, as the Rudolphs discovered on their first visit, shared the city block with five other similar buildings. Each was serviced by three lifts, five maids and one large rubbish tip. Tar-strip paths and paved quadrangles connected the buildings; the quadrangles were marked with keep-off signs. Clearly, the space was not intended as a playground for children. Three blocks away, up towards the city centre, the technical college was located. Walking downhill in the afternoons, the Reverend conjectured on Mrs Rudolph's behalf, it would take Annemarie no more than ten minutes to reach home. For the time being, though, to facilitate the removal, Annemarie delayed her registration until the winter.

Their leaving Merrydale was unceremonious. Annemarie bade no one farewell. Some of the girls in my class at school will be at the college, she told the Reverend the day the removal vans came, as though to account for sitting on the verandah with nothing to do and no one to see. Eager to agree, he was nodding his head even as she started to speak.

With similar nods and blinks he also syncopated Sylvie's words. In his presence she mused out loud. She would have called Mrs William Thomas of the History Society and people at the church, she assured him, had she not felt so conscious of her shame. She knew she must be imagining things, yet she heard her shame named whenever she went out in public. The first time Sylvie informed him of this fear, the Reverend advanced their house-moving date by a month.

The Rudolphs left their lounge suite with its new linen upholstery in the Merrydale house; they also abandoned the boxes in the attic. Sylvie felt that the living-room in the flat would be too small to take all their things. To herself she said it would be better to start anew and without bad memories. If she was in the living-room alone and looked just to the side of the armchairs, she could see her recent unhappiness crouched there against the backrests, settled in amongst the cushions. These hauntings, she hoped, would stick with the furniture and leave her at rest.

On the final day of the removal, the Reverend drove Sylvie over to the flat to supervise the carrying of her boxes of china. Once there, she decided not to return with him to spend the last night in Merrydale. Up in the flat, Sylvie said, she felt safe – she had not felt so safe in many weeks. Tell Annemarie, she instructed the Reverend, to eat the pie that had been bought for supper and not to forget to throw out the leftovers. Sylvie would busy herself here in the flat making things ready for tomorrow.

Though in the following weeks she would speak often of their new comfort and security, would praise the Reverend's name as she moved from window to window looking out, Sylvie at first made very little effort to settle into the flat. Her attempts to unpack were desultory. Mostly she sat in the centre of the empty new living-room remarking on the signs of use and wear left by previous tenants. She noticed that children had lived here, lots of little ones who had scuffed the floors and marked the walls. Their mother could have had no discipline; she had certainly lacked taste. Look at the wallpaper she had chosen. The loud protea pattern, especially against that back wall, reminded Sylvie at night, in the orange glow of the streetlight, of the bloated faces of dissolute burgomasters. The lily motifs in the bathroom were as bad, though in another way. To someone who wasn't looking too closely they looked very like dirty smears. When she had time again, at the first opportunity, she would have to find something more suitable.

So Sylvie chatted, conversationally and by the hour, addressing her remarks to Annemarie in an adjoining room.

'It's good to keep my voice exercised,' she observed, 'for when you, small Annemarie, go to the college. Because then I'll have no one to talk to.'

Sylvie had resumed the diminutive a few days after their move. Now, when Annemarie entered the room, Sylvie no longer kept her eyes fixed on whatever it was she might be doing. Sometimes, especially if Annemarie came in slowly without startling her, Sylvie beckoned her over. They had been in the flat three weeks the day Sylvie drew Annemarie close and pressed her head against her daughter's side.

'You're still my own Annemarie, aren't you?' she said. 'I wanted to tell you how well I think you organised the whole business of the house-moving with the Reverend. I'm so grateful to you both. What a good kind man the Reverend is. Dear and kind.'

The Reverend had made Sylvie over to a colleague of his in Hoopstad. A meeting between them was effected before Sylvie discovered that, amongst other things, the new Reverend lacked the Reverend Guthrie's sweet tooth. At the end of the afternoon encounter, the Reverend Doherty, large of jaw, broad of chest, well advanced into his middle age, addressed his hostess from the side of her secretaire. His fists were planted firmly upon the flap top. The Reverend Doherty, bent over slightly to press his point, promised Mrs Rudolph that things would surely work out better next time. When eating his lunch, he would remember to leave a space for cake. As Mrs Rudolph did not immediately respond to this idea, he gave up excuses and tried a little humour. He said that, apart from its spiritual meaning, he had found there was a personal gustatory appeal for him in that pungent phrase from the Book, 'the salt of the earth'.

'Oh, but I'm afraid I do so like my sweet things,' Sylvie confessed in return. 'All things sweet. A little sugar does no one any harm.'

'All true, Mrs Rudolph,' said the Reverend Doherty, straightening up and slipping a programme of parish events on to the secretaire. 'All true. Next time, as I say, I promise to try some of your cake. I look forward to it.'

Sylvie drew her arms across her breast.

'So do I, Reverend,' she said. 'No visit is complete without something good to eat.'

To ward off the grim prospect of the long emptiness of Saturdays, Sylvie bestowed upon the Reverend Guthrie a final tea, one of the very weightiest of her spreads. On a three-tiered tray were layered pound cake and her special extra-dense banana bread buttered with real dairy butter. On the top level Sylvie had balanced a high pile of butterfly cakes, still the Reverend's favourites, decorated with cherries and whipped cream. The Reverend, pipe in hand, called the display a feast such as any prince might come home to. Sylvie, crumbling bits of cake into her serviette, did not reply. Her glottis, she could feel, was glued shut.

They drew out their time together. Sylvie had the feeling of spreading out the minutes as she might creases in fabric when ironing. It was the first time that Sylvie had explicitly asked Annemarie to leave her alone with the Reverend at tea. Sylvie watched the Reverend take butterfly cake after butterfly cake, each time carefully prising out the inserted cherry with delicate motions of his tongue and then sucking out the cream. Squares of afternoon sunlight cast by the windows stretched and arched across the walls. For a long while they did not speak. Sylvie could hear the chewed cake move in the Reverend's mouth.

'It is so quiet in here,' she finally remarked. 'So peaceful. You chose so well, Reverend. Children don't play in the yard; there is no garden; no threat from the elements. Absolutely nothing to worry about.'

'I'm sure you'll be happy here,' said the Reverend, his reassuring tones smoothed by their swaddling of cake. He swallowed hard. So did Sylvie; she was noiselessly following the motions of his lips with her own.

'I'm also sure things will sort themselves out with Anne-marie,' he said. 'I have seen how subdued she has grown. Your distress has affected her. And the move will help matters. As we have seen, decent people live in this neighbourhood. You two can live here quietly and safely. You will be happy.'

'I will,' said Sylvie, adamant.

'The Lord will keep you.'

'He will.'

'Now let us pray.'

Unlike the many other times that they had prayed together, Sylvie today could not think up responses. The Reverend opened his eyes early to check if she was all right. She motioned with her head for him to proceed – she was following. She continued watching him after he had again bowed his head. She found she was making no meaning from anything he was saying. Her regret at his leaving was distracting her. It had occurred to her that her prayers from now on would be very alone. Would she be able to pray as effectively as before? The Reverend was good and was God's man; she had liked to hold his memory in her mind when praying – the image of him as he sat beside her on the verandah in Merrydale, and also the memory of his carefully chosen and spoken words. If she imagined she was in conversation with him, there was no fear of lacking the words to pray. The Reverend's words were warm upon her like the wind of spirit. Now she felt them; he was close beside her. She wished he might go on and on.

'Amen,' said the Reverend suddenly, on a falling tone, because his stomach pressing fast against his lungs was inhibiting speech.

'Lord, Amen,' agreed Sylvie, closing her eyes as he opened his.

Annemarie, sitting on her bed in her room, waiting for the diapason of their prayer's final moments – his urgent syllables measured by her mother's single affirmative exhalations – but they seemed to have left that bit out this time. She went to lie down on her bed, to pretend she was sleeping should the Reverend want to say goodbye. Sylvie, however, did not come to call her. Annemarie heard Sylvie in the kitchen, transferring the contents of the three-tiered tray to a Tupperware box for the Reverend's Sunday evening coffee. Annemarie heard him at the door, blessing their new home and then wishing Sylvie well. He was thudding his foot against the doorjamb. Sylvie sighed her gratitude.

When the lock snapped to behind him, Sylvie began to sigh louder, in shorter gasps. Annemarie thought she should go out, if only to stand beside her. She followed Sylvie to her bedroom door; in the doorway Sylvie turned. She was holding a tissue right over her face, up to the eyes, as though she had an injury to hide.

'Leave me,' Sylvie said from behind the tissue. 'I want to be alone. What I have to suffer sometimes feels too huge to bear.'

PART THREE

The barracks layout of the Rudolphs' flat compound repeated itself across the greater surface area of Hoopstad. In rows and columns of colonial red brick, low wide buildings filled the grid of the tarred streets. In certain ways Hoopstad was an enlarged Merrydale. There was a police station fenced in by an aloe hedge, and a large bus depot, tarred in this case and adjoining the railway station. Both the railway and the police stations were built of red brick. There was a wide main street, once designed for ox wagons. More recently, the city council had considered constructing islands of kikuyu grass down its middle. The islands were to be decorated by clumps of pincushion proteas. Because of the rapid expansion of Hoopstad, however, it was finally decided that tarred space should not be limited. As in Merrydale, beyond the business area of town, with its new shopping mall in brick and glass, there stretched the suburbs, where the pools were very blue, the gardens very wide, and the whitewash very white. On the other side of the city, across the hills – conveniently situated for ready access, but as conveniently hidden – was the township. It might be imagined that here too the grid and brick pattern dominated.

Yet, unlike Merrydale, Hoopstad was also a place of some provincial importance. In the city centre most of the street intersections were marked by traffic lights, and most of the central city blocks were occupied by official buildings: the tax office, the telephone exchange, the post office, the court. These were all built long and low and in brick, without much window space, like the police and railway stations. The largest buildings in Hoopstad were the brickworks and the chocolate factory, but these were off on the municipal limits, close to the old town graveyard.

The Hoopstad city brickworks projected to the sky three tall funnels of blackened brick, emitting considerable amounts of dark smoke, which liked to settle. Every morning at eight and every evening at five, every weekday, the same also pressed the city into the service of its siren, which repeated the first rising shriek of an air raid signal three times. To this summons of its workers, the citizens of Hoopstad set their clocks, shut up their shops, or thought of dinner. For those who might lack timepieces, the sound divided the official day, which was work, from the night, which was sleep. The siren, it should perhaps be added, was almost as audible across the hills as it was in the city.

The chocolate factory was less obtrusive. Its façade, which was painted in peppermint green-and-white stripes, was screened by a row of tall poplar trees, their brittle branches weighted down with brick dust. It was only on Fridays, when it was said they made the filling for nougat bars, that the citizens of Hoopstad were reminded of the existence of the chocolate factory. If the wind was blowing in the right direction, the city air was pervaded by the fragrance of honey. The fragrance penetrated even into the offices of councillors, receivers of revenue and police commandants, causing their mouths to pucker in an unconscious anticipation of stickiness. On very windy days, but much diluted by the distance and open-plan sewage works, the fragrance found its way also across the hills. Then children would raise their noses to the wind, the better to savour the sweetness it carried.

In Hoopstad I was bored. From the very beginning there seemed to be nothing to do. The problem lay in the way the two new facts of my existence worked together: spending my time, as far as possible, in Mother's company; and being without my journal. In the municipal dumping grounds in Merrydale, wedged under a pile of grey matter in which the parts of a pram and a smashed mess of beer cans might be distinguished, my journal notebooks had been stowed away. I did not regret the loss. I did not want to possess nor even again to read what Mother had read about me. For the time being, I reckoned, it was best to set the journal to one side.

But without the daily activity of writing the journal, time was unmemorable. As I no longer named and separated the days as they passed, whole weeks went by unnoticed and had no substance. Before, on the pages of the journal, I had made my time. Even when I lost interest in creating stories, I had gone on recording the passing of days. Transcribing newspaper passages, I had noted down dates and filled them in. Now I kept note neither of general facts nor of private fictions. I did not begin another journal. It felt like there was nothing to record. In the flat nothing much happened – Mother and I spent the days keeping one another company, and the city outside the flat seemed very remote.

I spent, as before, a great deal of time in my bedroom. But it was different now – I didn't want to be there. I stayed in my bedroom because the rest of the flat was Mother's space. I usually sat facing the door, with the door open. Mother could see me sitting there as she went up and down carrying books and ornaments, arranging things. But she did not much seem to want to look in as she passed – that was another difference. In a way the purpose of my being there – the Reverend's idea of the two of us being companionable – had no point. Now it was Mother's turn to be alone. She spent a lot of time praying. I heard her from my bedroom, speaking out loud and at length in her own.

Yet she seemed to want me in the vicinity. As the weeks went by she beckoned to me more often for brief reassuring hugs – quick pressures of forehead to breast – though she remained uncomfortable with me that close, would soon turn to one side, shaking her head and clicking her tongue and speaking of forgotten tasks. She talked to me from other rooms: chatted about the fresh taste of the water in Hoopstad or the early dryness of the autumn air. She wondered aloud whether it wasn't wiser to finally give way, confess one's laziness, and employ a maid. She spent several days trying to find the right hanging space for her large mirror with the gilt frame. To and fro she walked, from the bedroom to the hall and back again, hugging the mirror to her and asking if I had any good suggestions. But beyond this our intimacy did not go. She spoke only about general matters and in a distracted way, as though watching herself gesticulating in her glass.

For all that, though, we were never long out of one another's company: she did not go out, nor did I. No one came to visit; we might not have left Merrydale. The only difference was that our reclusiveness here felt more alone – we were very by ourselves. Now I no longer went to school and Mother did not resume those interests which in the past year she had cultivated. The Church, she said, is not the same without the

Reverend; and Hoopstad, as anyone with half an eye for culture can see, lacks history. It is surely a lot better for us to stay at home, while both of us have the chance. There are lots of things you can do here: you can read, you can learn – reading at home, you learn more than you ever would elsewhere. In her voice there was that partly winsome, partly plaintive expression with which she had made assertions of our closeness in the past. I fell in with her plans. When we went out, it was together, and mainly to supermarkets – the ones which were closest and small and where dust collected on the tins of baked beans and jars of piccalilli. Neither Mother nor I was comfortable in Hoopstad: the streets were wider and noisier; the pavements were packed tight with people; it was difficult to know how to push through.

Once, during the first week in Hoopstad, I went out alone and without warning Mother, to have a look at the local library. When I returned, I found her waiting at the door, her lips compressed to whiteness, her arms braced high across her breast. She had phoned the Reverend; they had prayed together on the phone. She had phoned the corner store where I bought bread and milk. She was just about to call the police.

'Where have you been?' she said so quietly I could barely hear the words. She paused only for breath, not to hear me make a reply. 'Never do this again,' she continued on the same undertone. 'Enough has happened. I repeat, never do this again. I must know where you go.'

But I had no intention of going anywhere. I stayed at home. Mother and I unpacked boxes and arranged furniture. And then rearranged what we had arranged. As the flat was smaller than the house, we repacked some things. In the afternoons I learned to knit. Each in our own room, Mother and I spent many hours knitting together. As we knitted, we would have the radio on, the plays and the chamber music, never the news. Mother turned off the radio at news time. As the pips came on, she said, 'Too much that's bad happens,' and cut them short. So we also watched less TV – Mother said it showed the bad in the world too clearly. Often we picnicked in front of the radio, plastic trays on paper napkins spread over poised knees. We did not have much appetite and Mother said she did not feel like cooking any more, yet, though it was in small amounts, we ate almost continuously. Mother's cheeks softened and sagged; her inner arms quivered as she knitted. I, on the other hand, grew thinner: the veins elbowed more prominently through the skin of my hands and temples. Being afraid that Mother might discover them, I had stopped taking diet pills at Christmas. Instead, I had learned to puke without retching and without mess, at least four times a day.

But extra time remained. We set ourselves reading tasks. There were books of Father's which neither of us had yet touched: Churchill's history of the Second World War, Robert Bridges and Edmund Blunden anthologies, biographies of Disraeli and Galsworthy and de Gaulle. We also read many novels, acquired mainly from the shop where we bought the bread and milk. Mother stressed that we should keep pace with one another, novel for novel, in order to have proper to-and-fro talks when we sat together to eat or to knit. But in spite of all this we still caught ourselves staring out of the windows a great deal. By day, when you looked out, you saw the expansive and unfamiliar blankness of the sky; at night there was the equally unfamiliar brilliance of the streetlights. Standing at the window, I fancied that the lights of the city from above must look like a giant illuminated knitting pattern – the thick cables of shopping streets here, an open rib design further out, stretched on the landscape up to where the city met the dark.

*   *   *

At night, Sylvie would sometimes pray at the window. When prayer was difficult, as it often was without the Reverend's presence and help, she looked out at the lights of the neighbourhood. If they had left their curtains open, she could see what the people in the nearby flats were doing. She watched the old woman sleeping in an armchair in the flat opposite. Her head was always hanging over to one side – had she slept in that position all her life? She watched the architects – a man-and-wife team, probably – in the flat just beneath the old woman's, the two young people who stood at their drawing tables and worked and spoke without ever looking up, at least as far as Sylvie could make out. If there was no one to watch she still stared out: there was a lot that was new to look at from the window – the buses moving along the lines of receding streetlights; the two sets of traffic lights, at two points of the flat block, changing just out of time. On cloudy nights there was also the spectacle of the city glow, a brilliant orange inflammation in the low sky. Sometimes Sylvie stared out so long that, when she lay down to sleep, she still seemed to see the lights bright before her, the rows and blocks of them: a grid of burning points pricked out on the inside of her lids. It was very different here from Merrydale and the unmixed darkness of John's view. It was not only the profusion of light but the ordered plan of the city: you knew at any minute where in space you were, who and what was around you.

Sylvie was not surprised she felt more at a distance from John in her new flat. Nothing here, other than photographs and a few pieces of furniture, reminded her of him; it was not even the kind of home he would have chosen. There was none of the open space they had in Merrydale and there was no view. She still missed him – of course she missed him – but in her imagination she could not place him here. Instead she thought about the Reverend. When the desolation of

January came back to her, she remembered his last visit. At such times the distance between Merrydale and Hoopstad seemed very great.

A photograph of the Reverend in a clear plastic standard stood on her dressing table, almost exactly beneath the picture of John that had hung in the living-room in Merrydale. Beside the photograph she placed the pot of African violets he had brought to their last tea. He had said – it was a small detail but important – that purple was his favourite colour, the colour of distant mountains and dark storm clouds over the African veld. She had said – they had been laughing – thanks to you, I will now appreciate that beauty of storm clouds and nature enraged, but without the worry. It has only been my pleasure, he had said, smiling gallantly into her face.

On her bedside table Sylvie erected a second shrine. Beside her Bible and the stinkwood cross mounted on its yellowwood base was a stoppered glazed glass bottle, as high as a hand. It had been her mother's, an old eau-de-Cologne bottle, perhaps. Sylvie made it her reliquary. This way, she decided, she could also keep the thought of John present to her, even in an unfamiliar place. Since they had come to the city, which was where the province cremated its citizens, Sylvie had sent for John's ashes. A pinch or two, with crumblings of dried alyssum flowers saved from the scorched Merrydale flower-beds, she carefully trickled into the bottle. The bulk of the ashes stood in their urn in her clothes cupboard. Later, when she and Annemarie were more settled, she might decide what to do with them.

But settling in was a slow process, no matter how secure and enclosed you might feel. Or perhaps it was not the settling in alone – it was also the effort of getting to feel comfortable with Annemarie again. The Reverend had impressed upon her that it would take time – perhaps many months, he said

– before her heart would grow whole again and before Annemarie would no longer feel like a stranger, would become once again her very own. Anxiety stayed with Sylvie: the initial aversion to Annemarie's body had, in a kind of contradictory way, set off the growing apprehension that, after what had happened, Annemarie might be wanting to leave home. The child gave no outward signs – except for the inordinate amount of time she spent staring out of the window – but when she chose to go alone to the shops, or when she strolled around the flat with nothing to do, Sylvie wondered if she was thinking about leaving. Sylvie began once again to listen for Annemarie's movements. Some days, even when she was praying in her bedroom, Sylvie would try to guess by the sounds she was making what Annemarie was doing next door. If she heard Annemarie bestirring herself, Sylvie would prepare to go out to join her. Often this meant running into Annemarie in the passage as though it were accidental. On each occasion, Sylvie tried to feign surprise.

'I'm off to sit by the window in the living-room for a while to knit. There's more light there than in my room,' said Annemarie one afternoon, walking past Sylvie as she poked her head around her bedroom door.

'Ah, I thought you were already in the living-room,' said Sylvie. 'You've been so quiet. How is the jersey, Annemarie? Is the difficult bit still giving you trouble?'

'I've finished that piece now. Look. What do you think?'

Annemarie stretched out a length of cross-hatched arm. Sylvie came closer to look. She bent low over the knitting. She was tracing out the line of the pattern with her finger. She was longing to extend her hand and hold Annemarie's wrist. She often had this feeling, most often at night when they called goodnight to each other from bed to bed. But she was afraid of approaching Annemarie head-on. She didn't want to look at her too long. She might again see how the child had appeared to her in the new year. She would see how the mouth was cut across the face in a fixed and startled wince. She would see the red flesh cooked by sun and shame, the eyes boiled to hardness.

Sylvie looked for ways of forgetting her fears; she thought that, if the Reverend telephoned, she would feel proud to sound stronger. The most helpful thing she decided to do was to shut out world news as much as possible. She had never really found it important, but now she didn't pay attention to radio reports and newspapers at all. There was enough distress to deal with, here, close at hand, in her own life, without having to go through public listings of disasters. She also put off joining societies. The idea had crept upon her during the last days in Merrydale that societies were no more than a forum for local and town gossip. As for a history group, Hoopstad was too new a place to create interest in the past. You got more information by reading.

But, as the year went on, a potential disturbance in the form of her broker threatened Sylvie's careful peace. At the best of times a retiring man, he was now forced to break his silence because of interesting new developments on the stock exchange. To the knowing eye, he solemnly told Sylvie on the telephone, forcing his high vowels, promise was everywhere to be espied. Treasures were accruing; money was spinning over into gold. Sylvie pulled out the telephone plug. So the broker sent telegrams. Sylvie then instructed him by letter to do as he saw fit. She wrote that John had trusted him; John had trusted also to the solid fortunes of this country. She said that she too trusted both. What was happening was a fulfilment of John's word.

Sylvie may have avoided the news of it, but she could not

entirely ignore her new wealth. John would have smiled –
his odd rare nipped-in smile – at these dividend figures.
Now, as never before, not even during the months after John's
death, she had the power to buy new things. There was the
living-room to fill up, the walls to repaper. She began to use
the empty pages of her old accounts book as scrap paper for
shopping lists. One day she took Annemarie with her to shop
for the house. They took the bus in to the huge new furniture
warehouse in the city centre. Sylvie found it was fun looking
at goods in Annemarie's company. They liked the same sorts
of sofas and armchairs: rotund ones, with bolster armrests.
They ordered a new suite on the spot. Close to the warehouse
was a delicatessen. They stopped to buy a cheesecake for
supper and a bag of mixed nuts to share. The nuts were still
warm from roasting so they ate them right there at the counter.
Sylvie held the packet in her cupped hands and Annemarie
picked out the walnuts for her because they were her favourites. Annemarie popped the nuts into Sylvie's mouth.

As they waited at the bus stop to go home, Sylvie spied a
craft store across the road that carried wallpaper. Sylvie
thought the Jugendstil designs displayed in the window might
suit. Annemarie agreed. They found – how very convenient
it was – that there was a sale on. Annemarie paged through
the samples on offer. Sylvie explored further afield. In the
cut-price racks filled with Chinese fans, plastic prayer wheels
and leather belts, she discovered boxes of do-it-yourself
mobiles: bits and shreds of wood chip, feather, reed and glass
to string together in her spare time.

'Annemarie,' Sylvie called her, 'look, we can make these
up ourselves. Won't that be something nice to do? You can
imagine how pretty they'll be.'

Annemarie came to stand beside her, taking two of the
mobile boxes from her hands.

'We could start tonight,' Sylvie continued. 'I'll make egg-nog – you know, the egg-nog I used to make. We could add a tiny dash of rum. We could hang all the mobiles we make in front of the living- and dining-room windows. It will fill up all that empty sky space.'

Sylvie piled several more boxes into the crook of her arm.

'So many, Mother?' Annemarie asked.

'Yes,' said Sylvie, choosing one more, a box that was shown to contain a mobile of bumble bees in fiery red gauze and wire. 'It doesn't matter. They'll be so pretty. Come, let's get all of these. We could start doing them tonight.'

The mobiles, complete with glue and explicit instructions, did not take long to make. They hung them in place along the curtain rail in the living-room to dry. In the morning, seeing the light on them, Sylvie was enchanted.

'That's exactly what the window needed,' she cried. 'What pretty things. Look at them dance in the sun! Do you see what I mean, small Annemarie? They relieve that wide expanse of empty sky. Such pretty things, don't you think?'

Annemarie came in from the next room.

Angular and sinuous, the mobiles were gamelan dancers in the sun. They recoiled, sprang. A fly was tossed off its flight path.

'They are pretty,' Annemarie agreed. 'They are nice to watch. Sort of mesmerising. You can imagine babies being fascinated.'

'Invalids, too,' said Sylvie. 'When they don't feel like reading, or are tired of gazing away into space.'

As it happened the mobiles came to fulfil the function Sylvie described. With the first chilling of the dry season, Sylvie fell ill. Her system, it was clear, had been overstrained. Her whole body ached. Worse than that, though, her May menstruation did not come. She reached inside herself for reassurance, to check for a chapping or a peeling that might mean the onset of old age. Though she felt as usual, she could not suppress the suspicion that she would not bleed again. She fell into reveries – the kind she had experienced during her pregnancy – trying to listen into her innards' stirrings. There was little response. She bought earplugs, the better to hear her blood surge and the glugging of her gut. The earplugs were a good idea – this way she could also avoid hearing Annemarie wandering around and about the flat. In this way, at least, she found more quietness. She remained pleased with her earplugs until the day the headache began. It lasted for days. She removed the plugs lest her head burst with the volume of its pain. She could not imagine how the skull contained it. At about the same time, or so it felt, her womb began to ache. Her whole mother-part seemed to want to sever company with her body. Her gut was wracked with the strain. Within a few hours, she retreated to the far corner of her bed, where she sat holding and rocking her belly. Annemarie went off to find a late-night chemist. By the time she returned, Sylvie had made it to the telephone to call a doctor.

The doctor who came was their first visitor since the departure of the Reverend. He was a small, soft-fleshed man called Howe, the thickness of whose nose was matched by the pendulous heaviness of his earlobes. Sylvie requested that Annemarie not be present at the consultation.

'It is important to me that she believes me not to be very ill, Doctor,' she explained.

'You are not very ill, Mrs Rudolph. My concern is that this kind of grippe with complications can be uncomfortable enough to warrant my telling her how to nurse you.'

'Yes, Doctor, of course I agree with you. It is the other thing, though, you understand, that I would prefer her not to know.'

'To her it will also happen one day.'

Sylvie bit her lips.

'This migraine holds on with steel pincers,' she said.

Annemarie offered the doctor a cup of tea before he left. Seated in an armchair, his knees drawn up, his body snugly folded, the doctor hardly needed to raise his hand to his lips in order to reach his tea.

'Do you think I will have to cancel my college enrolment again if her sickness continues?' Annemarie asked.

The doctor's eyes, magnified behind their pebble spectacles, moved hither and thither about the room before he spoke.

'Not necessarily,' he said. 'Not necessarily. What do you do now?'

'Nothing,' said Annemarie.

'Nothing?'

'I spend time with my mother.'

The doctor's retort was immediate and unblinking. 'You should get out a bit,' he said. 'Especially now while your mother is ill. It's no good to be in the sickbay all day.'

'She may worry,' said Annemarie.

The doctor took a breath, drawing in the corners of his lips so firmly that his cheeks and throat simultaneously puffed out.

'I will call round to see you and your mother tomorrow,' he said.

Annemarie spent the next morning in Sylvie's room. The sun lay in hot patches on the floor. The windows, holding squares of bright, blank sky were snowy television screens without pictures. The bedclothes steamed out the close odours of swaddled warmth and long-clothed flesh. Sylvie lay propped up against three pillows, holding a hot-water bottle to her abdomen, her eyes closed. Annemarie read out aloud from a

Georgette Heyer novel. Every half hour or so, when she went to refill the hot-water bottle, Annemarie also made fresh camomile tea. Every two hours, Sylvie had a steam bath in bed, to release the sinus that the doctor believed was the primary cause of her headache. The morning passed in peaceable companionship. At noon, when the sky began to burn, Sylvie suggested that, to give her a break from reading, Annemarie transfer some of the mobiles from the living-room to the bedroom window.

'If I have to spend many days in bed, it will be lovely to have them to look at,' she said.

Annemarie carried them through, one by one, to prevent their knotting.

'Hang them in the same order as before,' Sylvie instructed. 'The lighter, delicate ones on the one end, the heavier ones on the other, and with even space between. Start with the feathered one on the left, where there's least wind.'

'I was thinking that we should perhaps have this glass one in the middle, where it will catch the most light. See how striking it is,' said Annemarie.

'Yes. That's a good idea. I like to watch that one.'

Standing on a chair, Annemarie suspended the mobiles in their right spaces. Sylvie watched her.

'You're too thin, Annemarie,' she said. 'From where I am, I can see your hip bones protruding. Even from behind.'

'I eat enough,' said Annemarie.

'All I am saying is that you must be careful. You don't want to fall ill as well. Look at what happened to me. My system was telling me to take things easy.'

'I'm OK,' said Annemarie.

'You've become a great help to me, my little one,' Sylvie next said.

The perfective felt easier when Annemarie's back was turned.

'I'm glad you think so, Mother,' said Annemarie.

'In fact,' said Sylvie, taking a long breath, her eyes fixed on the nape of Annemarie's neck, 'I am very loath to see you go off to college, come next month.'

'Next month is close,' Annemarie agreed, hanging the last mobile, one made of cardboard turtle doves and gold foil suns.

'It's been good for me having you around. It has helped me. You know, I'm sure I fell ill just to have you pamper me. I've only worried a little that you might have been bored doing all this.' Sylvie drew the bedclothes up to her chin. 'Oh, that's the prettiest,' she quickly added, for Annemarie's back was turning.

'I've been OK,' said Annemarie.

'If you stayed around a little longer, I'd soon be better, I'm sure,' said Sylvie.

'Yes,' said Annemarie.

'I've also been thinking, little one, that it would probably be bad for both of us if you had to go out every day right now and attend college. You know, just when things were coming right.' Sylvie spoke in louder tones because Annemarie had moved off to the kitchen with their empty tea mugs and the hot-water bottle. 'June is too soon.'

'Yes, Mother,' Annemarie called out across the passage. 'But delaying another six months might be a little too long. From the point of view of the college, that is.'

'I will so miss you,' said Sylvie, more quietly, as though to someone standing close to her bed.

'What was that?' Annemarie called. 'The kettle is boiling. I can't hear you.'

She came back in bearing a plate of digestive biscuits for lunch.

'Look,' she said, holding out the plate before setting it down on the tea table wheeled up against the bedside cabinet.

'Some of your favourites. The ones you most like dipping.'

Sylvie did not respond immediately, she was staring down the length of the bed. She inhaled so deeply, the breath caught in her throat. She clasped her lower abdomen with two hands. 'I just don't want you to leave me yet,' she said. 'I mean, if you don't too much mind spending time with me. If it helps, you could think of being with me as a kind of job. It's been done before, women being each other's companions – sisters living together, or mothers and daughters.'

Annemarie sat down beside her, in the curve of her mother's hip.

'If the college let me, I could defer again,' she said. 'Yes. I suppose I could. But, if I do, perhaps I should get some part-time work. You know, something very temporary, just to tide me over and to get out a bit. What do you think? Would you feel all right about that?'

Sylvie drew herself up against her pillows. 'Let's think about it before making a final decision,' she said. 'But I do honestly mean what I say. I would like you to stay and keep me company. It really would help me. I can't tell you how much it would.'

Dr Howe returned that night. After checking up on Sylvie he again came to have tea with Annemarie. He sat in the same chair as before, tucking up his body. For a while he said nothing. He drank his tea hot, blowing the steam away in sharp puffs. Annemarie watched him. She noticed his spectacles were so thick, they reflected arcs of green and purple light. She made a comment about the mobiles – how they'd shifted them to the bedroom, how Mother liked watching them – but met with no response. Sweat dripped off the doctor's nose into his tea.

'You should open the windows more,' Dr Howe finally said. 'Even though it's winter, it's warm enough.'

Annemarie still sat gazing at him, thinking that in some odd way his bald imperatives matched the impassivity of his fleshy chin and cheeks.

'It's too close in here,' he continued.

'Mother feels the draught,' said Annemarie. 'That's why the windows are closed.'

'I did a little asking around and it turns out I have just the thing for you,' Dr Howe then said, without a pause to signal the change of topic.

'Excuse me?' asked Annemarie, sitting up.

The doctor sucked up his remaining mouthful of tea, swilled round the leaves in the cup, threw back his head and let the last drops trickle down into his pursed lips. He scrutinised the inside of the cup for lingering residue.

'Work,' he said. 'I think you should do some work. It would be a way of getting out more, getting some air.'

'I would, I suppose, if I could do something not completely full-time, you know. If I had time left over to spend with my mother.'

'Yes, I'm aware of that,' said the doctor. 'That's why I mention it. There's a clinic, you see, that I help at, the Myburgh Clinic, out on the factory side of town. At the moment they are in need of volunteers, to do the admin. You'll understand that their resources are not vast. They depend largely on donations and voluntary services. But the place is very necessary – it fulfils a vital function in the community. They could do with the time you have available.'

'I have never heard of this place,' said Annemarie.

'I would have assumed that,' said the doctor. 'Obviously you wouldn't have.' He was wiping his face and pate with a handkerchief. As he wiped the skin seemed to glow more brightly. 'You also won't know much about the work itself. But you can learn. It won't take long. And I think it's a good opportunity. You will learn a great deal.'

'I must speak to my mother,' said Annemarie.

'Yes, you must. Of course you must. I'll put in a good word for you, too,' said the doctor. 'We could say it's a good cause.'

He might have been giving a half-suppressed smile, but Annemarie could not be sure.

'Is it?' she asked.

'You could put it that way. If you wanted to.'

'It's for the blacks, then?'

'For those who are objects of charity from the likes of us? Well, yes, it's for the blacks. Exactly right.'

Annemarie heard only his affirmative tone.

'I'm interested,' she said. 'Only please don't tell Mother it's for the blacks. Not right away anyway. I will, later on, when she's more used to the idea of me working. It might all be a bit sudden for her at first.'

'I wasn't planning to give her those kind of details,' said Dr Howe. 'I was thinking of raising the matter in a very general way when I see her tomorrow. In the meantime, though, you should call the clinic.'

He got up to leave. Annemarie followed him to the door. He paused there to write his telephone number and the number of the clinic on a piece of prescription paper. When Annemarie stepped forward to close and lock the flat door behind him, she felt, quite tangibly, because her feet were bare, that he had warmed the floor where he had stood. This, she decided, was a good sign.

After about six months – though that way of saying it is inaccurate, time then being of a thick and even consistency like albumen, and, like albumen, resisting through-movement – after about six months, the situation in the flat changed a little. Through the unexpected intervention of her doctor,

Mother and I reached a compromise: we decided, in a way, to divide time between us. A clinic, where the doctor himself sometimes worked, required volunteer helpers to perform secretarial tasks. He suggested I apply.

The doctor's suggestion did not displease Mother. As the job didn't look too much like a real job, she told me, I would, in all probability, still be spending plenty of time at home. The plan also satisfied me. I had the feeling – a robust, positive feeling – that this might somehow be a lucky break-through. It was the kind of work I had long been hoping for – doing a generous turn, stretching out to the unfortunate, working to mend and make anew. If I succeeded, I thought, aware somewhere inside me of a distinct sensation of triumph, Simon's discouragement would come to be nothing more than a temporary setback. I could prove that lending a hand was straightforward and honest after all, especially when, as any-one could see, people were in need of help. The point was again to recognise that wholeness was better than apartness. I might, I conceded to myself, be little more than a functionary, doing the clinic accounts with Sue and Marly. But that didn't make me any less of a helper. I would be serving those whom the clinic served; administering, even if at one remove, to the poor and sick and black.

The Myburgh Clinic building was a long low bungalow built of brick, in the style of much of Hoopstad. It had once been a mission hospital and after that a school. Different tones of brick marked the additions which had been made over the years. The building was now divided into four main areas. On the one side lay the maternity and child health wards; on the other the casualty and tuberculosis sections. Sue, Marly and I worked in a prefabricated cubicle of a room that had recently been constructed together with a row of toilets to the side of the main building. The offices proper had been taken over by the maternity section which, despite the expansion, was still full of babies.

The first day I arrived – in early June, in the early morning, the dust of the compound pressed hard by frost – Sue gave me a quick tour round the place. It was the last time I was to see its inside walls for several months. From the short broad passage which bisected the building Sue led me out on to the verandah running along its length at the back. The verandah was open to the outside; folding doors connected it with each one of the wards. On warm days, Sue explained, patients could sit out here to catch some sun. For a while we stood in the sun ourselves, watching the glitter of the frost disappear off the ground. We heard a bell ring back at the office, steps clatter down the passage.

'It's funny, you know,' said Sue, starting to walk on. 'Sometimes this place still feels to me as much a school as it does a clinic. Or does from our point of view in the office. The nursing staff probably wouldn't agree.'

From the office window as I worked I could see only the narrow side of the main building, a square of brick without windows. One day, after being at the clinic about a month, I again walked round to the back, to have another look at things. The compound here was no more than a bare space of trodden earth. A line of wattle trees ran down the inside of the whitewashed wall that divided the clinic land from the open veld. Some afternoons, Sue had explained, people lined up in the shade for outpatients' treatment. Today there was no one. I was disappointed. I walked down the length of the verandah. At the entrance to the main passage, a group of people, some of them staff, were standing together talking. I nodded at them. They appeared not to see me. There were very few people sitting out today, it being winter, almost cold and very dusty.

At the far end of the building, in that section of the verandah corresponding to the casualty division, I noticed a young man sitting alone. He appeared to be of about Simon's age and build: from a distance you could fool yourself into seeing a resemblance. I went up closer to check. It was difficult to make sure of the man's features. He kept his head well down and his body hunched. He was hugging his knees to his chest, his palms flush with his ribs. His shirt hung open. I saw that he was bandaged from his armpits to his waist.

I stood alongside him, hoping to attract his attention. It wasn't Simon, but I thought I should be friendly. He did not look up. I said hello, loudly and conspicuously. He still kept his head down. For something to do, I walked across the compound to the boundary fence. Though the staff group had gone in and no one was looking at me, I felt a little spare. When I turned back, the young man was getting up. He and I walked together – nearly in step – along the length of the verandah to the door. He did not change his pace, neither to get beyond nor behind me. As we were walking in time, I hoped he might at last look up to acknowledge my presence. I kept my eyes on him. But his head remained well down.

That was a Monday. On Tuesday Dr Howe called me from his practice in town. It was almost lunch-time; I was tidying my desk before leaving work. Dr Howe's voice on the telephone sounded thick, as though he was dragging his tongue.

'You were seen wandering around the clinic grounds yesterday,' he said. 'Don't do it again.'

'I'm sorry,' I said, blushing to myself. 'I wanted to see what was going on. I'm interested.'

'We each have our own place in the clinic organisation,' he said. 'If we all try to get involved with more than what has been assigned to us then we won't know where we are. You are a part-time volunteer worker.'

'I know. I just wanted to see a little more of the place.'

'That will happen, Annemarie. In due course. For the moment you should concentrate on simply getting to know your side of the work.'

'It was my time off.' I paused for a breath. 'I have plenty of time on my hands. I could do more work. I mean, be more useful.'

'Annemarie, you must remember, or perhaps learn, that the clinic is not a charitable organisation.' The doctor was talking more insistently, but also more quietly – he seemed to be holding the mouthpiece closer to his lips. 'The clinic is not there to cure social ills. It is simply a clinic – it is for sick people. More than that we are under pressure simply to keep running as a clinic. A place like that – because of who it serves and where it stands – is vulnerable. It exists only because of governmental good grace and our good services. So we operate from day to day to provide those basic services. Nothing more. And we perform those tasks by observing due limits. You must learn to accept that.'

'I'm sorry,' I said again, blushing again, rotating my chair away from Sue and Marly. I turned my teacup in its saucer. I half hoped he might go on. 'Thank you very – ' I began to say, but he had hung up.

I left work a little earlier that day. Instead of going by bus, as I usually did, I took the extra time, before Mother would be expecting me, to walk home along the back and side streets of town.

The road back to town from the clinic led past the chocolate factory. As I walked down the line of poplars which divided factory land from kerb, I tried measuring the distance between the trees in footsteps. From the bus the trees seemed very evenly spaced, their parallel lines corresponding exactly to the striped effect of the factory façade. I found the trees were evenly spaced in reality also. Dust gathered on my legs and dress as I walked. Each time I set down a foot, it seemed, a clump of kerb grass dissolved into a flurry of dust.

Between the chocolate factory and the railway station I crossed a new subdivision of council housing that was being marked out on the veld. Lines of lamp post and wire fencing and stormwater guttering anticipated the onset of more concrete structures. It looked like you could wheel them in – park your house. One prospective house owner, thinking of tomorrow, had already set up a new bright-black wrought iron gate. A sign wired to its top spike told me to beware of the dog. Whoever it was was taking precautions. With all this strangely empty space around you could see why, though; Mother certainly would see why. You could very easily feel nervous, wondering where the people and the houses were.

I came upon the Hoopstad bus depot without having really intended to; I had not thought it lay on this side of town from the railway station. I was surprised by the clamour and the movement after the openness of the newly developed land. Unlike Merrydale there were more buses here, also more people and fewer trees. But there was as much dust, despite the tarmac. I stood on the pavement by the side of the road leading out of town. The smile of a black model much pleased with a new brand of heavy-duty soap gaped from a billboard above my head. Around me people were forming and re-forming into small circles and queues. Everyone seemed to be talking all at the same time. They all, it occurred to me, had someone with whom to talk. I felt alone and out of place. Then I thought their voices might be enveloping the crowd in its own enclosing pockets of noise. That was why no one noticed me. I remembered Mother was sitting indoors at the flat, in silence, listening to the stillness and the radio. She would be waiting. In front of her were the mobiles creating quiet spaces for their own movement. Perhaps I should go home.

Dust was coating my throat and I began to cough. I strained my eyes to penetrate the dust. I found I could see across to the straight horizon that divided the city from the township. What happened over there? Until Sue had told me, I had not known that was where the township was. Sue had explained that most of the population of Hoopstad lived over there. Finding things out seemed so difficult. What could the place be like? I walked a little way in that direction. Buses kept coming in and leaving, interrupting my view. If I took a bus – say I took a bus – how would it be? How could I ask what to do? If no one would look at me, that is. What would I do once there? Yet I should not forget that Mother might even now be worrying. I'd like to see the place, though. You never knew. Perhaps Biko, Barney Pityana, others – the leaders I had read about – had spoken there, here, close to Hoopstad, in the early days. You could never know. What would the place be like – the kind of hall where they met, the house where they stayed? If only you could go over and see. A bus stopped directly in front of me, breathing exhaust and dust. I turned back.

I found a child – thin and in a too-big dress – had come to stand in front of me. When she caught my eye she asked for money. I shook my head and began to walk on. She followed me a little way, repeating, 'Ten cents, ten cents,' over and over, wistfully, but without hope. After a block, as I reached the first shopping street, the Indian stores, I turned to explain to her that the money my mother had given me that morning I had used to buy lunch. I crouched down and explained at length. She gazed at me uncomprehendingly, waited till I had finished speaking, then said again, 'Ten cents.'

I felt I should start to hurry. There was the thought of Mother at the kitchen window, waiting. She was listening for my step in the passageway. She would wonder about my dust-scuffed shoes. She would want to take me to the bathroom and lave my cheeks and then praise me for my work. I quickened my pace. The child dropped back in the pavement crowd. I pressed my bag against my hip, to check that it was still closed and full.

Though your vision is sliced into strips by the blinds – which are down, to give shade, but open to allow light to enter – you can see into the office if you come quite close. You may do so undisturbed. For the moment, it being just past one, there is no one in the room. The secretaries have gone to lunch. Sure enough, on one of the desks stands an open empty lunch box. Another of the secretaries tidied her hair before lunch. Beside her typewriter lies an orange comb.

Life can't be that bad here. Two electric fans have been provided. They stand in a corner, heads ducked down, coyly observing each other. In a few months' time it will indeed get warm beneath this corrugated iron. But not for the time being – it is still early September. On the walls are a few bright posters. There is a picture – bird's-eye shot in fish-eye vision – of the entire province, taken from the sea on a clear day. This version appeared one Saturday on the centrefold of the main provincial newspaper. It is fading, though: the blues and greens, which make up most of the picture, are almost indistinguishable. A pity. Next to the picture hangs a food chart, showing the constituents of a balanced diet. The meat and fresh fruit are well featured. They are brightest. The large wall calendar supplied by a local butcher in this area is closest to the door. It bears the picture of a young girl feeding geese. Here too the blues and greens are fading, but not as much so. The girl's white skin and pink dress stand out clearly. It is the kind of calendar that comes with one picture only. The one picture becomes the rebus of the year. This is the year of the goose girl.

You can tell which is Annemarie's desk. Not by the fact that it has the least amount of paper on it – though that fact is noteworthy – but because her bag is on the chair. You know that bag. It was purchased before Annemarie started this job – her very first job, though unpaid. In it, for you watch her kitting it out every morning, are a hairbrush, her purse, her Forestmist deodorant spray, her pocket money, and some tissues. The bag is open. That is careless of Annemarie. Even though most of the people – that is, not the secretaries, but those others – are here because they are indisposed and would not prowl around, it is foolish to take chances.

You move off to find Annemarie, for by now she must have taken leave of her colleagues for the day. How surprised she will be to see you here, come to pick her up, travelling all the way by bus to this dusty spot. Perhaps Annemarie will show her mother something of the rest of the place. How nice that would be. It would be interesting to observe a little of what is done – the things that the white man does for them. Unfortunately, there are no windows on this side of the clinic building; you cannot see in. It seems all in all a quiet place, though, decent and neat. The work is probably reasonable – the doctor said she would only be doing some typing and basic bookkeeping. It's true, yes, that the place is not entirely conventional; yes, it was a bit of a surprise learning about all the blacks around. But at the same time it's difficult to imagine how things could go badly off the rails. A clinic, no matter who it admits, is an institution: there are boundaries one must keep and duties to fulfil.

Next time you come you might take Annemarie out to lunch. Out here one can't help thinking of good things to eat. With the factory so close, the air on this side of town is saturated with nougat; thoughts run to sweetness. Annemarie says the factory has a small cafeteria attached to it, a kind of showcase for its sweetmeats. Something soft and creamy, in light pastry, would slide down quite easily right now – something like a plump but delicately textured custard slice. Perhaps Annemarie could be persuaded to come along even today, just for a surprise snack. And then next time they could make it a proper treat for her – a full meal of meat and gravy and dessert. Like a kind of reward for all the voluntary labour: a way of saying keep up with all the good work.

Sylvie was not yet completely well, but she did feel a lot better. Because she had not started bleeding again and thought she should take it easy – just in case she might – she still spent her afternoons resting in bed, but at the same time she felt much stronger and more able. It was probably, she thought to herself, the inspiriting influence on both their lives of Annemarie's new work. Sylvie was wholeheartedly in support of the project, she explained to the Reverend on the telephone. It was a healthy plan of action, would probably keep them both busy, and the idea had come from their new family doctor, a kindly, tubby man whom you simply trusted on sight. Annemarie had also agreed to go out to work only twice a week which, remembering that she was working half-days, meant she wouldn't be spending too much time away from home. So, taking everything together, Sylvie concluded, she, as her mother, could not but abet the girl.

Sylvie now set her handiwork to good purpose. She knitted and crocheted blankets, comforters and knee-wraps for the clinic. The jerseys she and Annemarie had produced over the past months she packed in boxes, which she sent first to the clinic and then also to local charities: the polio people, the palsy people, those who made the money for those who cared.

One early morning Sylvie called Dr Howe at his rooms to tell him about an idea she had for the clinic. It had all come to her the day before while knitting. She had been thinking, she explained, that they should institute a reward scheme at the clinic whereby deserving patients, say those who best co-operated with staff, were given blankets to take home. It was important, you see, of course the doctor would understand, to spread the available warmth as widely as possible. In fact, once you began this kind of work, Sylvie added, you suddenly began to perceive all kinds of ways in which charity could work – you could imagine nets of helping hands stretched across the country; and then you began to want to help as much as you could. Dr Howe, his voice deep in his throat, waited till she had finished, then said thank you very much for the idea; your blankets would come in very handy, Mrs Rudolph; I will put your proposal before the steering committee in due course.

Sylvie found ways of helping Annemarie more directly. Every Monday and Tuesday, when Annemarie got home from work, Sylvie took her off to the bathroom to sponge down her face and dab cucumber lotion on her cheeks and neck and forehead. You could hardly believe how dusty the girl was. It was truly admirable, her doing so much for others – that is, for the blacks. On a few occasions, when she felt up to it, Sylvie took the bus right out to the clinic and treated Annemarie to lunch. They usually went to the cafeteria at the factory, where the chocolate salesmen ate together with their managers, and sometimes to the Portuguese tea-room which was closer to town. They would spend an hour, then travel home together. This way Sylvie got an idea of where her blankets went, and what kind of work Annemarie was actually doing. She got an even clearer idea when Annemarie brought home end-of-the-month rush jobs. She asked to help; Anne-marie said yes, she might. They would sit together at the dining-room table, working in silence.

Sylvie rediscovered the afternoon contentment of Saturdays – almost the same kind of feeling as she had experienced in the old days with the Reverend. She sat in bed knitting, cosy and comfortable. Tea was on the tea table, with cake and cookies – firm evidence that Annemarie was learning to bake correctly from the book. One day, Sylvie thought, they should get round to unpacking the cookbooks that still lay stored in the boxes underneath her bed and in the spare bedroom cupboard. Sylvie's hands followed of their own accord the knitting patterns propped on her knee. She was free to watch the mobiles against the sun. She had added to her collection, not only in this room but also in the living-room and even in the kitchen. She could see no harm in it: the mobiles gave you such simple visual pleasure. When she had exhausted the stock at the craft store, Sylvie sent away to wholesale suppliers for more of the same – lots more pretty gingly-forms in different shapes and colours. Did they have more of the make-it-yourself mobile packs on offer or in the pipeline, Sylvie wrote, more of the attractive glass kind, especially, the different prism formations; or of the feather varieties, the ones that came in cloud and angel and swan shapes?

Sylvie found she could watch them all day. The elegant light-winged wind-tapped things. Before each window in the flat she had suspended them. With every movement of the air they linked arms, twisted, flew. Annemarie agreed to introduce two to her office – both of them in abstract shapes; one in folded reed, one in perspex discs. She hung them in the office window. She said they looked just right, and Marly thought them lovely.

*   *   *

There is a flash flat fashion in mobiles. Miss Eccles, the retired botanist who lives in the flat below, has, on her way to the washing lines on the roof, spied the decorative show of Mrs Rudolph's kitchen and spare bedroom windows, the windows that face on to the public passageways. Even her maid has commented on the display, Miss Eccles reports to the Flat Social Committee: 'What is it, missus?' was what her maid had said. Inspired, Miss Eccles has dared to approach the lady who has the mobiles, whom you rarely see out. As it turns out, she's actually quite prepared to chat. Miss Eccles and the lady have now exchanged mobile notions and also knitting patterns. Imagine, the lady has a daughter who works for charity – yes, the thin retiring girl who you see coming home at lunch-time. Apparently both mother and daughter choose to spend most of their time at home. Miss Eccles has passed some mobile suggestions – we should all do it, think of the general effect – not only to Mrs Damson, Co-ordinating Secretary of the Flat Social Committee, but also to deaf Mrs Porterhouse who lives in the block opposite and who sometimes comes to meetings. The lady – Sylvie Rudolph her name is – doesn't mind people copying her idea. She has told Miss Eccles that even the tall, unsmiling man who is her neighbour – the one who walks by the kitchen window on his way to work and back each day – well, apparently even he has fixed his eyes on the dancing balances in her windows. And has, on occasion, stopped to stare. When Mrs Rudolph told the tale, Miss Eccles reports, she blushed a little. As well she might, says Mrs Damson, what with all this attention. He seems a very private man, the Flat Social Committee agrees. But never fear, says Miss Eccles when she and Mrs Rudolph meet in the passageway, we will get him to hang a mobile yet.

*　　*　　*

145

There is a face turned into the window at eight in the morning and at five-thirty in the afternoon. Sylvie Rudolph keeps noticing the turning. She tries a smile. Day after day she tries it. In this way she finally succeeds in meeting her neighbour.

Congruous beauty of the human form, unyielding to the telling flaw, bears the still, clear proportions of a crafted thing. In the honed, untrammelled spaces of the beautiful face, admiration lingers tremulous. Terror lies in this symmetry – how can it hold? The worshipper wants only to touch the image with her eyes, but is afraid. Can this beauty be? When the object of beauty turns to hold her gaze, will the face be a human face: softer, more porous, perhaps even blinking?

Beauty which seems ideal but is of the world imposes its presence upon the senses. Of Dr Étienne Roux, when they first meet him, people immediately say, 'He is the most beautiful man I have ever seen.' The force of the impression is located primarily in the eyes. Dr Roux's eyes are of a pale luminous brown, almost ochre, set in cavernous sockets, and, by virtue of the contrast, arresting. The bones of the face, like those of the rest of the body, are heavy and prominent, giving the effect of strength under restraint, but never of grossness. Precision of form sets off the massiveness. The lines of throat, thigh and spine run straight, are nowhere muddled. It is a body that cannot but end in an expertly turned foot – the tendons tense and strong, the fine instep balancing the fullness of the toes. The hands give the same effect: the fingers, though thick, are long, the nail beds chiselled; on the broad palms the lines run thin, but deep.

Dr Roux's beauty allows him to adopt an unapproachable mien. While his face dominates attention, he seems to withdraw behind it. His expression is immobile, the better to be observed, the better also to hide thought. This immobility gives Dr Roux the power of surprise. His vacant thoughtful gaze may spring into sudden focus. The observer, discomfited, looks away. But the direct light of Dr Roux's eyes, though preventing more absorbed contemplation, demands a return. The observer must watch the eyes, the eyes only. Giving the effect of strong fluorescence, the eyes now focus the face. Fixed by their gaze, the one who observed forgets the Doctor's beauty.

Dr Étienne Roux strikes those who first meet him with the magnitude of his knowledge. He holds degrees from universities in two of the country's capitals. He has gone abroad on scholarship. He has spoken at conferences in America and in Europe. The Doctor's field is political science. His doctorate dealt with executive autonomy in the constitutional order. The Doctor is without a doubt a cognoscente. His idle interest is in the early eighteenth century, the music and the architecture of the period. He is concerned about the corruption of sensibility in the modern age and discusses it frequently. Any group of listeners might become an audience for his views. Already arrested by the physical presence, people will be drawn by the meditative flow of his voice. Dr Roux speaks in the interrogative, inviting response but always intercepting it. He speaks to develop a topic, answering his own questions with further questions, but his audience is included by his tone, his searching glance and the interest of his anecdote. In conversation, the Doctor has the power to allow them silence, without their ever feeling ill at ease.

Whereas his knowledge and perception equip him for the official duties of his job, Dr Roux's proficiency as a causeur is valuable for any operational strategy he might devise, both for his serious and for his less formal work. His job demands that Dr Roux talk to dignitaries, cult figures and figureheads, to heroes, flunkeys and traitors. Recently, he has even stopped to talk to Mrs Rudolph, who is a housewife and his next-door neighbour. He talks in small-town prisons, and state rooms, and living-rooms where the *braai* stands smoking outside. But for the same reason that he talks to develop an idea or to prove a point, Dr Roux can also keep silent. This is when his expression remains impassive, when for hours he keeps very still, waiting now for the answers from his interlocutor. Dr Roux drives a white Audi across the length and breadth of the country. He is immaculately barbered, wears tailor-made suits and collects antique snuff boxes. Seven years ago he divorced his wife. She was later murdered by her second husband. He no longer keeps a photograph of her. Dr Roux has started to hold conversations in the lift with Mrs Rudolph because the wax paper butterfly mobile which hangs in her kitchen window reminds him of the one his mother hung above his cot bed when he was very young. That was before he learned to speak.

On a sheet of mauve writing paper, gold-dusted, shirred and scalloped at the edges, specially bought by Sylvie, Annemarie has Marly write out the menu in her neat, chubby cursive. 'Vichyssoise', she spells, and Marly forms the letters.

'Roast shoulder of lamb. New potatoes. Baby peas and carrots in butter,' she recites from memory, and Marly, tongue between teeth, murmurs assent.

'Nègre en chemise. Mille-feuilles,' she enumerates.

Marly unclamps her tongue and licks her lips.

'Then coffee, filter coffee, and those after-dinner soft-centred coffee chocolates you can buy, instead of mints,' she adds, addressing Sue who has joined them.

Marly, her eyes closed, is transported.

Sue says, 'She really hasn't forgotten a thing, has she? She really knows how to do it.'

'Invite us some time,' says Marly, reading over what she has written. 'This sounds like heaven.'

'It's my mother's first attempt in ages.'

'So you must be expecting a special guest,' Sue observes.

'It's our neighbour who's coming,' says Annemarie. 'But it's for the first time. He's a doctor of some kind.'

'Well, well,' says Marly. 'He must be quite special.'

Sue walks over to her desk. She glances out of the window. 'There are people queueing over at the clinic,' she says. 'That means they're starting work again. Come on, you two. Lunch-time is over.'

PART FOUR

Sylvie Rudolph is having Dr Étienne Roux to dinner. She has foraged in the spare bedroom for her best cookery books. She is planning a *mélange* of familiar fare, such as to make the man feel at home, combined with some French furbelows, for he is a lover of culture, and oriented to things European. The occasion for the dinner is her purchase of a new forty-eight-piece dinner service, sprigged with an imitation Meissen motif, but the impulse to have a party came during the last and longest conversation she had with Dr Roux. This conversation moved from the lift and along the passage to her living-room sofa, and dwelt at first on the deterioration of music programmes on the radio, and, in general, the problems of nurturing culture in a land of dark barbarians. Sylvie decided she liked to hear him talk.

Dr Roux will arrive at eight. At five the white carnations will arrive for the table centrepiece. All morning Sylvie will spend giving the flat its first thorough cleaning in months. Dr Roux looks like a man who likes the look of house pride. She will rest in the afternoon, to collect her strength. Annemarie will prepare the vegetables and the table. Sylvie has already been to a new hairdresser, recommended by Marly, whom Sylvie has befriended. As Marly points out, a caring and careful hairdresser makes a woman feel her best. Sylvie wants to be at her best tonight, for the Doctor is a man of taste, versed in the arts of refinement. She has purchased a new blouse for Annemarie. She has also purchased a new blouse for herself, in undyed raw silk. Both are imports from Italy. The Doctor is a man of Europe, and has a discriminating eye. Sylvie hopes he will make this the first of many visits. That he will become a familiar guest. It may be her role in life to coddle the gustation of lone good men, to offer them sustenance and make them pleased. It is true that even the best amongst us need companionship. With pleasure Sylvie thinks of what she will serve at dinner: the warmed cream in the soup, the soft white rolls and the emolliated chocolate – good things to fold comfort around the body core.

Despite the Doctor's presumed powers of discernment, Sylvie does not feel too nervous on the night. She knows she will be at home with a man who appreciates tasty cuisine tastefully appointed. Annemarie and the oven are co-operating. The vichyssoise is blending. For the first time since the new year, when she pauses to check on what she is feeling and what her body is telling her, Sylvie senses neither apprehension nor pain. The mobiles hang motionless and lovely in every window. It is a still evening. In the carnation arrangement Sylvie has inserted feather snowflakes left over from mobile making. On the radio, for a change, is one of her favourite sonatas. With each breath she takes, Sylvie feels more buoyant.

*　　*　　*

'This is an opus,' said Dr Roux, after I had set down the dessert – the lucent interleavings, the plump darkness peaked with white. As he spoke, he stretched out his hands, the palms open, to either side, to my mother and to me. 'And these are the presiding spirits of the household,' he added.

Though the wine he had brought already bloomed fiercely in her cheeks, Mother's colour darkened. She may have ducked her head. My eyes were held by the spectacle of his beauty.

I was aware of my body as corporeal, as brute matter displacing space, as I had been once before, the time after I met the man at the mountain resort. I was sweating. I could feel my nose and chin jutting forwards, my fingers and toes protruding from my hot hands and feet. The air was teasing out my body hair. My hair lay across my shoulders, folded warm as a shawl, combed and spread by Mother.

Mother had asked me to participate in her grooming.

'Annemarie.' She sought my attention, pulling at the back pleats of her new blouse, squinting askance at her profile. 'Aren't you excited? I had forgotten this feeling. It's like being girls again, isn't it? Isn't it fabulous?'

She had scrubbed my back in the bath; it was the first time in months. It felt as though my skin were roughly, newly exposed. I was shy. Though she kept calling, I dressed in my own room. I did not want her eyes to return to my body – the flesh reddened and puckered by the hot water, the awkward wickerwork of bones.

She insisted on brushing my hair. She stretched it out with a fine comb, watching us both in the mirror.

'Let it shine,' she said, bending down to reach the ends. 'Let it shine.'

She applied lipstick to my lips, miming with her mouth how I was to spread the red fat.

'Isn't this a lovely colour?' she asked, turning the stick in its holder. 'It's called Inner Crimson – as in a rose.'

She leant into the mirror to apply her own, pausing at each quick touch to glance down the flank of each jaw.

'Mother,' I found the words to tease, 'he is at least ten years your junior.'

Her face came round, indignant. She was dark against the bright lamps of the mirror. Her voice rose and quailed.

'Annemarie, you didn't say that,' she enjoined me. 'You know it isn't like that at all. How could you think it? He is simply a man of civilised taste – whose company I would value. That means we should try not to offend him.'

I backed away. My face, receding in the mirror, circled the round 'O' of my red mouth.

But the excitement was burning in her. She was close up to the mirror again, checking from this angle and that the even spread of her make-up. Her fingers trembled over her face.

The same trembling – a concentrated nervous energy – expressed itself here in the atmosphere around the dinner table: it lay behind the precision operation of the meal; it lived in the fringes of light around the candle flames, the tableware, our cheeks. It lay like an offering also in the Doctor's upturned palms, the strange tension between their attitude of receiving and the tautness of his wrist and fingers – their suggestion of reaching.

For some time there had been no conversation. Mother got up to make coffee.

'Dr Roux?' she said, bending towards him in an implied request for permission.

'Étienne,' he said, turning over the hand closest to her to pat the table.

'Étienne,' she said, pursing her lips, almost dimpling.

Her lipstick blurred the contours of her mouth. Below the nose it was smudged; around the corners the colour had bled.

In the mirror above the dresser, in the half-light, her mouth was a bruised cut.

'Coffee?' she asked. And when he nodded, 'How do you take it?'

'Black,' he said, with relish. 'Dark, black and bitter.'

'Just as I like it,' said Mother, though it was a lie.

As she went out to the kitchen, he turned to me.

'I hear from your mother that you have a job,' he stated. With his eyes full upon me, my own gaze faltered. It crossed my mind that in the full light of his eyes his face was not as beautiful.

'Only part-time volunteer work,' I said.

'Our house doctor organised it,' said Mother, coming in with coffee cups.

His eyes were still directed at me. I felt I should say a little more.

'It's at the Myburgh Clinic,' I said.

'I have heard of it,' said the Doctor. 'Medical students lend a hand there, don't they?'

'Yes, as do the general practitioners from town. But there is still a shortage of doctors.'

'At least there is a clinic, though,' said Mother, bringing in coffee. 'At least we continue to find ways of helping those people.' She looked to the Doctor for affirmation. But his eyes had not yet relaxed their hold on my face.

'What else do you do?' he asked, after a thoughtful pause.

'She keeps me company,' said Mother hastily. 'You know how these children are when they first leave school. They don't know what they want. They need to wait, to think about what they want to be.'

The Doctor had dropped his eyes to watch the coffee curl into his cup.

'Yes,' he softly pronounced, though his quiet tone seemed to be contradicted by the clenching of his hands as he pushed himself back from the table. His chair scraped on the floor.

'We take too little time in this day and age for thought, even for meditation,' he went on. I saw Mother's gaze grow vague as she concentrated on his words. 'In wiser times, men considered their actions; their lives were not unpremeditated, they paused before doing or speaking. Nothing was without its due constraint.'

It was his longest speech yet. As he warmed to it, I noticed for the first time his formality of enunciation.

Mother began telling him about the beneficial serenity that she obtained from praying, even though prayers themselves might achieve no direct results. The Doctor dovetailed his fists together on the table as he listened. I sat back a little, relieved at being temporarily released from his attention. The tension in the air, though, remained palpably present. I could hear Mother's breath catching, as though on a suppressed burp, at the end of each long sentence that she spoke. I worried that she might not be able to control the sound, that she might betray the stress of her excitement. I watched her in the mirror. It was only gradually that I became aware that Étienne Roux's eyes were, like mine, focused on the reflection. Perhaps he too had started by watching Mother. However it was, we had each of us been observing the other askance for some time before we caught each other at it. This way of putting it, though, is misleading, implying a sudden simul-taneous recognition of mutual awareness – perhaps a quick, almost sexual *frisson*. But there was nothing of this. There was only the apprehension, a sudden intensification of the sense of anxiety – or was it danger? – which had begun be-fore he arrived. It was so strong that I was sure Mother must feel it too. This was the source of her nervousness. I glanced back at her reflection. But she was still doggedly, implacably, talking about praying. And Dr Roux was nodding his encour-agement, while staring at me in the mirror. I turned my head quickly to avoid his eyes. He was faster. As I turned, he was bending down to pick up Mother's dropped napkin. One hand he left on the table as a balance. I realised I had never before seen such flesh; it looked glabrous, blanched – not so much naked, as immodestly bare.

The reiteration of the summer. Christmas and heat. Ribbed repeat patterns of mirages line the horizons of the streets. The wet dust is the colour of brick is the colour of the city. The stickiness of nougat is in the stickiness of the heat. It is Christmas in the city: galleries of tinsel under tungsten. In the warmth of the evenings parents march children in pyjamas and slippers along rows of hot shop windows, full of vivid shapes. In the humidity of suburban gardens, around the dripping tap and the swimming pool filter, mosquitoes swarm.

'What ever shall we do with all these patients?' says a doctor at the clinic. 'There are too many sick.'

On Saturday afternoons Étienne Roux and Sylvie drive to the city on the coast to hear symphony concerts. They return with frangipani crushed beneath their soles, humming themes. One afternoon Étienne takes his new Nikon along with him. That evening two exposures are left. Annemarie takes one of him and Sylvie, shoulder to shoulder. They blink as the flash explodes. Miss Eccles takes the other, of the three of them out in the passage. Annemarie and Étienne each have a hand on Sylvie's arms. They all are smiling. The light burns in their eyes. Though Sylvie giggles and simpers – how silly we'll look – Annemarie asks Étienne to give her a copy.

In the heat the mobiles wilt, fade, tilt. Annemarie watches them. One Saturday afternoon when she is alone, she removes the ones which hang at her bedroom window, each with a perpendicular downward tug – like grabbing nettles. Miss Eccles and Mrs Damson, having tea in Miss Eccles's flat, telephone her to come over. While your mother is out, they suggest. Annemarie is agitated. Thank you, but I have so much to do, she tells them.

The office fans at the Myburgh Clinic overheat, flap out of time – gammy wings. The septic tank is stewing. Though there remains more sweetness in the air than shit, disease breeds fast as cockroaches. Staff are away.

'Give me something to do, I have nothing to do,' says Annemarie.

'This weekend – Saturday especially – we could do with extra help. The casualty people will have a lot on their hands. It's often like this over Christmas and New Year,' says Dr Howe.

He phones Sylvie to request her permission.

It is the swilling of slops, bejewelled brightness of blood and porridge-soft ruptures. Annemarie pukes all night and the next day – involuntarily now and between meals.

The student doctor who is Sue's friend says knowingly, 'There is plenty of work here, plenty of work, when you know where to look.' Multiple excrescences of acne bedeck his neck and cheeks. Two nipple-moles poke through his hair. 'There are too many sick people for us to cope with,' he says.

It is Christmas dinner at Sylvie's. It is in the heat of the day. There are more candles, carnations, more cream than ever before. Like weary caryatids the candles bend. The menu is as long as ever; its calligraphic flourishes are finer – Dr Roux has rendered them in a sinuous cursive. The guest list is mostly as one might predict: Sylvie, Annemarie, Étienne, the Reverend Guthrie (who sent his apologies – who has gone home to his parents). There is one extra, not officially invited: Adrian, the student doctor with whom Annemarie has worked. He came in at the time of the entrées, to see if Annemarie could spare a few hours that night; he stayed to sample profiteroles, to forestall their deflating in the heat. Étienne stares at Adrian. Adrian blinks back, picks at his acne. Who is your friend? asks Étienne over coffee, after the young doctor has left. Annemarie looks befuddled; she has just been to the bathroom, where she has been forcefully relieving herself of food. Come, says Sylvie, hand on the coffee pot, profiterole stains on her chin, we should say our Christmas prayer.

You should not take on extra tasks, Sylvie regularly tells Annemarie, this is the festive season: it is time for revel and also rest. It will soon be the New Year, she says, sales will be on; we could make a day of shopping, like we did last year. Sylvie works her way through the department stores. She must find wool to knit Dr Roux a polo neck jersey for the winter. In the window of a shop called Afrikraft she discovers a new kind of ornament: miniature metallic jewel trees – like upended mobiles. They could decorate her bedside table and her secretaire; they could stand as focal features. She will treat herself to them.

She asks Annemarie where she should put the amethyst one, where the rose quartz. Annemarie is noncommittal. Your mind is not here with me, you have worked too hard, Sylvie again tells her. She will have to hold down a full-time job sometime, soothes Étienne, so let her do the work she wants to for the moment – especially if it keeps her out of mischief. All three laugh – polite hiccoughed giggles. Étienne makes as if to wink at Annemarie. The nod does not seem to interrupt his stare. On Sunday evenings Sylvie goes over to listen to music at Étienne's. He has a room specially appointed and proofed for refined sound. It is the room in his flat corresponding to Annemarie's in Sylvie's. Étienne brings in a chair to join the white leather sofa where he always sits. While the music plays they do not speak. Sylvie knits his polo jersey.

Next door Annemarie lies half asleep on the Sunday papers, sweetening her insides with diet drinks in traffic colours. Maybe Adrian will call on her again to help at the clinic. She will try not to think of what she has seen in the wards, the fresh wet wounds and the old streaming sores – eye-ache oddities of bodies in pain. If she remembers too clearly, she will want to refuse when he phones. She shouldn't do that, because the extra work is important. It helps the overtasked doctors. And of course the sick, too. Helping at the clinic, she also escapes her boredom. The festive season is long.

The first month of the new year, nineteen hundred and seventy-nine, brought the final close to a near year-long hebetant hiatus.

'Another year, the very last of this decade. Our last chance to right its course. Before the eighties come.'

Mother spoke the words on New Year's Eve in Étienne's music room.

Following her lead we raised glasses of Moët, keeping our paper plates of salmon toast poised on our knees.

Étienne turned down the volume knob on his TV. He spoke in place of the mouthing compère and the silenced revellers at the State Theatre celebration.

'We can but express the old hopes,' he said, holding his glass meditatively against the light. 'We hope of course for richness of all descriptions, and concord; for well-being and good governance. There is much matter for hope. On the national level we are ending the decade in a position of strength. And as citizens we may take our inspiration from this. We have every reason to look forward to the eighties.'

Looking at Mother's eyes raised now to Étienne's face, now to his glass in full expectation of further eloquence, I felt a reciprocal quickening of anticipation.

Étienne was at the stereo. He put on Beethoven's last symphony, the 'Ode an die Freude'.

'Hear this,' he said.

The music strained high, and higher, and took flight. It was possible to have all sorts of hope.

By the first week of January, I was back at the clinic office, but now as a full-time salaried employee. Sue had resigned quite suddenly at the start of the month; she had found a job in town as secretary to a legal firm. I moved over to her desk. A new secretary was employed, a black woman whose name now escapes me and which at the time I could not pronounce. I felt in place again, able, too. It was not like the few nights I had kept Adrian company in the wards. That was messy stuff; I had done nothing but fetch and carry and still had to take time to retch. This work I knew and could do. I did extra hours of it, into lunch-time and after four. Dr Howe left a gift on my desk, a carved soapstone hedgehog. It came with a note: 'Well done,' it said. 'Good work.' I was proud.

At the same time as starting the new job, I also began with extra work for Adrian, things he needed doing while he was away. This year, his house job complete, Adrian was based at the City Hospital. He visited the clinic only on Fridays, and sometimes, it was rumoured, also over the weekend. He called me – it became our term of telephone greeting – his secretary-in-residence. He had asked me to keep a look-out for him, that is, he explained, receive his calls, accept and collect his letters. Yes, I said immediately, of course, yes. But will you trust me, I added, seeing as I got so squeamish doing that other work? He plucked at the end of his nose – it was a habit of his – and did not reply. He gave me a cardboard box that had held carbolic soap to store his mail. I placed it next to the filing cabinet.

My task was hardly arduous, though I could not help wondering at the amount of material that piled up in the box. I discovered that many people came and asked for him. Few of them were ill. Some were orderlies with whom he had worked, but there were others. I thought they might be past patients wanting to pay their respects. They brought him mail – sometimes folded notes, sometimes large padded envelopes. They were mainly men, solitary men, who came walking slowly and purposefully down the road that led to the clinic. They knew where to find me, generally came right in after knocking, without hesitating at the door as official messengers might. Marly suggested I ask Adrian what was going on; he could not expect us to act as his personal staff. After that I began to distribute the mail from the box amongst my various lower desk drawers, so that Marly would not notice how much had built up over the week. I did not question helping Adrian: he had gone so far as to ask me for my help – had asked a second time even after I had shown weakness. I could at least try to do something useful in return.

In the New Year there was another development that boded well for the future. It had, of course, to do with Mother. It was her growing happiness, and the soft new light in her eyes.

I had told Mother about the job offer over tea in her bedroom. Étienne was present, sitting in the armchair by the window. Mother's chair was drawn up to his. Étienne was paging through her childhood photograph albums. His broad thumb stroked down the length of each vellum page as he turned it. She offered no comment on the pictures; they might have been those of an unknown third person. Her eyes followed his down the page, and every so often flicked up to his face, as though to make sure of his expression.

To tell my news I came to stand directly in front of them. Mother laid a detaining hand on Étienne's arm. He reciprocated her gaze, then closed the album. Together they turned their eyes on me. But neither of them voiced any objection. What had been spoken over Christmas regarding my work situation had been enough.

'It marks the end of our long lunches,' was the single regret Mother expressed. She leaned further forward to meet Étienne's gaze. 'I would sometimes pick Annemarie up for lunch last year, when she was doing half-days,' she explained. 'We had fun, didn't we, Annemarie?'

Dr Roux contracted his brows in a single symmetrical motion.

'I had not thought it was quite the place for lunch dates,' he said.

'Oh, it's not at all what you might imagine,' said Mother. 'The secretaries' office is quite separate from the clinic proper. It's like an ordinary work situation. And there are a few lunch places within reach by bus or car. Which reminds me. There's one thing you must promise me, Annemarie. Though you will be working afternoons, I want you to return from work before dark, or else telephone me.'

'The streets are crawling at that time,' the Doctor agreed. 'I avoid rush hour if I possibly can. It does help to work flexi-time.'

'That's what you should aim for in the next job you find, small Annemarie,' said Mother, her smile stretching wide enough to include Étienne also. 'When you work flexi-hours like the Doctor here you can take out extra time. Go to a midday concert or to the shops. Have tea.'

*   *   *

165

It is January 1979. Annemarie is working full time. Sylvie is happier than she has been in many years. Sylvie and Annemarie consolidate a friendship each.

One day

During the course of the afternoon a thunderstorm builds up. Sylvie is baking. She telephones Dr Roux, who, conveniently, is at home. He will do her the favour; he will pick Annemarie up from work.

As it is not yet raining, Annemarie is waiting at the clinic gates. Dr Roux gets out of his car to meet her, to carry her bag, open her door.

As they settle in, they sight a hand – a kinetic blur – waving from a window.

'That your friend?' asks Dr Roux.

'My friend?' asks Annemarie in turn.

'The one who came over on Christmas Day. Who works with you.'

'Oh, him,' says Annemarie. 'We never really worked together, you know. I only helped him out a few times – when things were busy over the Christmas period. And now he's no longer around much.'

The Doctor's profile is an elegant console for his dark glasses. He starts the car.

'You regret that?' he asks.

'I don't know, really. My time is pretty well taken up with the job I have at the moment.'

'I do admire you young people for the kind of work you do,' remarks the Doctor with some vigour in his voice.

'But compared to Adrian van Vuuren – that's my doctor friend – I do nothing at all. My job is really just a very ordinary job,' says Annemarie, watching the Doctor's hands.

The Doctor wields the wheel as though it were a pair of garden shears.

'It's almost too ordinary,' Annemarie adds.

'You think so?' he says.

He looks at her. With his eyes blanked out, the force of his beauty is full upon her.

'I'm sure you perform some very useful services,' he says after a while, his eyes back on the road.

Annemarie ducks her head in Sylvie's attitude of dimpling.

Another day

After almost one whole year in Hoopstad, Annemarie is out for the first time. Dr Adrian van Vuuren, whom she is getting to know at the clinic, has offered to give her a ride home. On the way they stop at a coffee shop, the Cumberland Coffee Shoppe: red gingham, stained paper napkins and, under domed plastic cake covers, clutches of bicarbonated biscuits and scones.

'An innocent enough place,' says Adrian.

They decide to have shortbread and tea. They find seats at the window which faces on to the street. Adrian connects fly spots on the glass and flips crumbs off the table as they speak.

'So it's the same old story,' Annemarie is explaining. She pours the tea. 'What I wanted to do then is the same as now – to help in some way.'

'Help?'

'Yes, help. As I said – to lighten what seems a burdensome situation.'

'On whose behalf?'

Adrian is fingering the long mole that comes through the hair above his left ear.

'I would think it was obvious.'

'Not really. The same old story, you say. So it might be for some. But only for some. The talk of fraternal love and peace is fairly exclusive. For a great number of people it doesn't

167

seem that easy. Things have changed and the rap is different. People are asking whose peace, whose love? Persuasive leaders have been asking those questions.'

There is an uncertain note in Annemarie's voice she tries to suppress by swallowing a gulp of tea.

'You mean someone like Biko?'

'Yes, of course, Biko. That's why he was silenced.'

Annemarie is looking out at the dispersing five-thirty crowd.

'Look.' She suddenly points, her finger against the glass. 'There's Étienne.'

'Étienne?' says Adrian, his attention again attracted to the fly spots. 'Who's Étienne?'

'You know, the man at my mother's Christmas dinner. Her friend. He told me he worked near here.'

'What a coincidence,' remarks Adrian without interest, bisecting a fly spot with his index nail.

'I still don't know what work it is he does, though,' says Annemarie sitting back.

'If I remember, he looked like a professional of some description,' says Adrian. 'Like me, you know. It's my sort of image,' he adds.

He nudges her foot with his. His lips turn down in an expression of sternness. Annemarie smiles.

That night Étienne comes over to ask Sylvie's advice on the best stock for clear soups.

'It's a good coffee shop,' he winks at Annemarie, who is knitting.

Annemarie drops two stitches.

*   *   *

A third day

In Etienne's flat, in the white music room, they have good red Cape wine and Strauss's last songs. Sylvie is seated on the white sofa this time, wanting to tuck up her legs. Étienne is standing, one long strong leg lightly crooked at the knee, one elbow planted on the supporting strut of the wall unit, his eyes musing on the Flaccati rug – a daguerreotype of the gentleman in his club.

'Annemarie's a good quiet girl.'

'Thank goodness.'

'Impressively quiet.'

'Yes. We've had our time of worry – it was very distressing – but we've weathered that. We put it down to growing pains and to her father's death.'

'Wonderful for you to be so close to her. Also to have her so physically close. Even with her new working hours. It's a unique situation.'

'It is,' says Sylvie. 'A year ago I might not have called it wonderful. But now – yes, I agree. It's wonderful and unique. As I was saying earlier, Étienne, I'm very thankful for everything that this last year has brought me.'

A fourth day

The clinic again. A warm evening. Banks of cloud. Not much light outside to see by. The office is in darkness; the day staff have gone home. Only that which is unusual stands out: the parked car, for example, Adrian van Vuuren's, close to the office, and the two people walking in darkness towards it. After getting into the car, they sit talking; their faces in profile, leaning towards one another, are in simultaneous animation. The car drives some way down the road; now stops against a graded kerb. Dust blows in the headlights, which stay on. In the middle distance is a large 'For Sale' sign in orange and white, just illuminated by the lights. The two in the car are

169

clearly silhouetted. Their heads come close together again, pause, meet. This time there is little talking. When the car drives off, the kerb is left eroded.

I will draw up a simple causal chain. It plots out the initial course of the new year.

In January my new job at the Myburgh Clinic began to take me away from home for whole consecutive days. In the set-up between Mother and me this was of course unprecedented. At about the same time I grew to be in love again – more seriously than I had been before. I was in love with the only young man I had met, the student doctor who helped at the clinic. And falling in love, remembering what had happened once before, I grew to feel anxious.

At this time Mother too was away from home more often, though usually at night, when she went out with Étienne. Most days she spent in the flat. She said she was making friends with Miss Eccles; she was once again trying out new recipes. She might, one day when she felt up to it, she said, play the piano again; her life was very full, full and content. But I did not take her entirely at her word. Because I was in love I was careful. When I went out to work I set watch upon my things.

I had not exchanged letters with anyone in a year. Adrian, who was not in love with me, did not send me love notes – so letters were not a worry. But I had to beware of other possibly telltale signs. It was essential to be cautious. Mother was newly happy – I should take pains not to alarm her. I should attempt to cover the traces of my emotion.

At the time I was looking through anthologies of poetry, especially Metaphysical poetry, to find correspondences with my own revived fervour. I began to check whether Mother was perhaps doing this reading along with me – during the day when I was not home. She well might, I thought to myself, remembering our reading programmes of the past year. To find out for sure I laid marks upon my books.

Once I left a hair on top of the book pile by my bed, a single hair, coiled into the shape of a treble clef. Another time I placed a bookmark at just such an angle beside a supine dead fly. The breeze was never permitted to blow through the flat in such a way as to disturb signs as light and subtle as these. So if I came back to find them disturbed, at least I would know Mother was again feeling curious about me – that she had perhaps sensed the warming of my new love.

I was surprised how much safer my surveillance scheme made me feel. I developed it. I got into the habit each morning of judging by squares of parquet, as though with graph paper, the angle at which I left my door ajar. Though Mother still came in to dust my room once or twice a week, I also made sure to have by heart the arrangement of pens and pencils in that familiar black mug, 'Our Dad', now transferred to my desk. If she stirred them about, just as if she entered and walked around the room, I would at once have seen it. The red pencil on the left would be off the perpendicular; the door would not be at the same angle. I would know she'd been in.

In an odd conniving kind of way I preferred to know that she was again watchful of me – if indeed she perceived my emotion – than withhold her from intruding. Watching was a silent, unobtrusive kind of thing; but a locked door or a spoken injunction might bring on the old pain in her breast. It was possible of course that what I was doing was unnecessary – it was possible Mother was not feeling suspicious at all. This way, though, the minute she picked up anything, I would know it.

When Adrian's offers of lifts home became more regular, and my hope grew more robust – in particular after the time when we spent part of an evening in his car feeling out each other's anatomy – I began to pay attention also to possible signs left in my clothes: sweat stains and blotches, dark scuff marks, excessive dust. I kept a picture in my mind of the exact mix of soiled underwear in my wash basket. That new year I insisted on a new project of doing my own washing. But the more I reiterated my plan, the more Mother stared at me hard, held out a hand in a gesture of supplication – she had learned it from Étienne – and remarked how puzzled all this made her. This was not another quirk, was it? she asked. Hadn't we got past that? Were it not for the general serenity in the air, she might almost have to start getting anxious all over again – yes, just ever so slightly. No mother, that is, none in her knowledge, she said, was put off by her daughter's intimate things. Mothers were there to be close to their daughters – that we knew by now. We weren't growing shy of each other's bodies, were we? No, Mother, no, of course, I agreed. But the work I was doing over Christmas, I added, had made me think. I was thinking that, as a part of offering to help others, maybe it was a good idea to learn to look after myself.

For a time after this conversation, if I tried to hide my laundry, Mother would search for it; under the bed and behind the cupboard, she inevitably found what I tried to bury. Almost I was persuaded to go back to the old system; her forages were not helping my peace of mind. But after a few weeks of such uninspiring toil she gave it up; I began again to leave the dirty things out, exposed but also marked; arranged each time in elaborate mosaic patterns – diaper and vesica and cusp designs. I never found these changed. Could it be that Mother had seen through what I was doing? That she saw the signs, studied their shapes and left them as she had found them? I decided it was impossible. I was sure I could detect the least signs of rummaging. I knew if she had been in, and, if so, if she had only been dusting.

So it was that by the end of February, on coming home at six, I developed an easiness in joining Mother and Étienne for gin and tonics. I came over straight from the front door, still carrying my bag; Étienne would pour my drink as I seated myself on the couch beside Mother to kiss her. Then with barely a pause, Étienne and Mother would resume their conversation. I would listen. I would watch the way Mother leaned forward if Étienne was speaking urgently, leaned back if he made only casual observations. Sometimes I joined in with them: the situation was relaxed. I would tell Mother and Étienne about work. Étienne was always interested in what was happening at the clinic. The main thing was that I no longer felt, as I had in January, that I should go first to my room – to put down my things, see how the place looked. I now had a way of keeping charge of it. I could rest in that knowledge.

It was around this time that Mother said to me one Sunday afternoon, 'You must have wondered before today what it is that Étienne does for a living.'

Her eyes were intent on my face.

'Yes,' she continued, watching for the expression she now seemed to see registered. 'I have also not been uninterested. A man so civilised, you'd expect him to be a somebody of some sort. Well, last night, during the champagne interval at the concert – not very nice champagne, by the way, though the music was out of this world – last night he finally enlightened me. I told him that, for my part, he need not have hesitated, but I did take his point that he needed to be careful. He said I should find the right time to tell you, that I should wait if necessary. But I couldn't think of a better time than the present, seeing that we're comfortable and together.'

It was, as it so often seemed to be, teatime in Mother's room. Though there was still enough blue in the sky, the bedside lamp was on, massaging warmth into the wooden cross and the cloudy glass vial of Father's ashes. Étienne had sent round petits fours in a candy-striped box. Mother had a plate half full of them on her knee.

'So, then, what is it that he does?' I said.

I seem to remember a pause here, but that could well be the result of remembering – a sort of syncopation for effect.

'He is a high-level intelligence officer. He works for the National Intelligence Service,' Mother then said.

Her gaze remained focused on my face.

'What does that mean?'

'He works at a very high level is mainly what I know. He has an extremely responsible position. But that was only to be expected. Étienne is a very gifted and able man. I would imagine that he works to catch out the cleverest of the people who try to upset the state of justice and order in the country – those who try to disrupt the nation. It is no secret that what we have in this country, the wealth and the civilised society, is coveted by others. Étienne watches, to make sure they don't have their way and take it from us.'

'You mean he works as a sort of national detective?'

'That's putting it too crudely. He's nothing sinister, of that we can be sure. Only yesterday he was telling me that various secret societies have tried to recruit him, but he has resisted them, sometimes at the expense of his own chances of promotion. Even without knowing him this long, I would implicitly believe him – a man so decent and refined. With someone like him around, we know we are in good hands.'

Mother absent-mindedly held out the plate of petits fours; I pressed it back, the stainless steel rim against my fingertips.

'Oh, I forgot for a minute,' said Mother. 'You still don't eat cakes.'

The day was losing light. Mother switched off the bedside lamp. The mobiles were displayed against the darkening sky.

As though a television had been switched on, we both turned to watch them.

'The point is this,' said Mother in the partially abstracted way that with her signalled the end of a conversation. 'Our flat has been proved even safer than it seemed before. We have now discovered that we have our own watchman next door.'

This may have been a joke, but I could not check her expression in the half-light. To disguise my own absence of laughter, I tried to speak in jest.

'We must be safe as houses,' I said.

Now Annemarie knows that her early exercises in paranoia were like playing games. Now she has nightmares. She wakes up sweating; damp is on her pelvis and chest. But she does not know exactly what she has dreamed.

She has some idea, though, of what she may have seen in her dreams. Because during the day startling new imaginings beset her. She suspects these are the continuation of the dreams.

Like film-clips stuck on the sprockets of thought – when she is typing or bathing or paring her nails – a series of images keeps recurring in her mind. In all of them, Étienne features prominently.

She sees that Étienne will come in through the open door of the bedroom. He will stand in the middle of the room, slowly turning from the window to the bed to face her. He will raise his hand – the large well-formed hand of a *kouros* – palm upwards, as though prompting her to rise. She will be sitting on the bed: knees together, hands on knees, team photograph style. She will remain sitting. She perceives Étienne's gesture is not aimed directly at her. The plane which the palm describes slopes down to the space beneath the bed.

What is it Étienne sees there? Or is it that he is looking for something? Is he seeking what he cannot see, but senses is hidden there? Étienne, says Mother, is very gifted. And Adrian has given Annemarie a suitcase for safekeeping. Does Étienne know the suitcase is there? Annemarie fears as much.

It was on Friday afternoon, the week before last, that Adrian gave her the case. He hadn't been round to talk in ten days. Now he came to tell her he would be away again, for a longer time, no more than a month, though. He asked would the case be a problem? Annemarie shook her head. He asked again, is she sure? Annemarie nodded, yes. It is difficult to reply because her queries cannot be spoken. Like, why he is so very often away? Is there any other help she can give him? She longs to see him more often. Not even to speak to him, like they did that day in the coffee shop – only to see him. But she can't tell him that. Her mouth won't say the words. So she handed over his mail – as always, a very big pack. He backed off. He didn't seem to want to go outside with her for a minute, as he sometimes did, when she would tell him about who had been round to see him. Now he was jamming his mail into his pocket as he took several steps towards the door, obviously letting her know he was in a hurry. He asked her for a third time, is she sure it's OK regarding the suitcase? The contents are not that important, but it would be a help. Annemarie tells him she is always willing to do him a service; she says she doesn't need to tell him that, he should know by now she likes to help out.

Now the suitcase is under Annemarie's bed; behind a bank of shoes and one old, moth-manged panda bear; the maw of a decrepit electric heater; a folded roll of old maroon carpet; a springform arm-and-leg trimmer that has sprung; two large tumbrel-shaped spools of wool, one green, one red, in a thick plastic bag that once held three; a soup tureen in a cardboard box marked soup tureen, one part of a forty-eight-piece dinner service not yet fully unpacked; and two books, a John Donne anthology and a calorie counter: behind these the suitcase lies hidden. Surely Étienne will not know that it is there. He cannot know. But why then does he stand with hand extended, the fluted finger surface just slightly convex with the strain of the pointing?

She will look away. It will be all right. Here, take my hand, the gesture could equally well be saying. Here, no weapon; no blighting eye in the orbit of this palm. Yet she can't do it. His gaze is demanding her attention. She follows the line of it, the lead of his hand. There is no way of ignoring what he wants. He insists upon it.

The fear relaxes her limbs. She feels the mattress depressed beneath her; she knows her body will give way. Sweat scratches between her legs. She must slap away his hand to make him drop his stare. She is unable. She will bend over, thorax to thighs; thighs open to insistent sternum; knees compressing chin. Her head will drop, her arms will drop down, her hands will point under the bed: here is a low tunnel, headroom only. She will look up: seek what you will.

And now she will be searching for him, and for her mother – the two of them together. They are in there, though they do not reply. She knows because there is music. Outside in the passage she calls in a loud voice. Because of the music they do not hear her. When she calls, knocking at his kitchen window, the glass mobile – it was given by Mother – is stirred by the reverberations.

She will try the door; she should have tried it before. It is unlocked. Inside all is voluminous harmony and the sweetness of honey. The air is compressed by a fever pitch of sound; 'Ode an die Freude' squeezes essences of nectar and nut. It is as though factory exhalations were here concentrated. Mother has been making almond fudge or maybe nougat, and Étienne is playing music for her.

The two of them will be in the white room. This door too opens to Annemarie's touch. She coughs on sweetness; there are tears in her eyes. But still she will see them clearly. Mother is on Étienne's white leather sofa; her legs are drawn in closely beneath her, folded like an origami shape. Étienne has pulled a chair up close. His hands hover solicitously over hers. She is dandling the objects on the glass-topped table. Jewel trees of amethyst, jasper and rose quartz she arranges small to large. Glass jars with clear plastic stoppers holding gold dust, lacquered beads, watch hands, ebony shavings, a metronome without a dial; a desk-top toy – black frame and five chrome balls – she holds, places, touches. Tapping his nail against the chrome edge of the table, Étienne speaks out the triumphal chorus theme. Mother looks up at him, joins in with him. Trying to find the pitch, her voice scratches across the harmony.

Annemarie will have to interrupt them. She will rush in. She will stand before them till they notice her and start up. Mother, Mother! Annemarie will cry above the sound of the music. Étienne! I will tell you everything. I have come to tell you everything! Listen to what I must say.

These imaginings will not let her go.

She will take the bus out of town, away to the township beyond the hills that she has never seen. The bus drops her off. She walks the road. It is very long. So long that the horizon comes no nearer, even when she quickens her pace. She might have known. Simon once warned her it was difficult to get close. Her shoes are heavy, her calves feel thin and stretched. She is covered in dust. What will Mother say?

The odd thing, though, is that there are people coming in the opposite direction, coming slowly but with purpose, marching in rows, in one long column that stretches back over the hills: a long march mainly of young people, people her age. What is happening? she will ask. What is the occasion? But no one listens to her. She stands forward; she is pressed to one side. She will try to join the end of the procession, but there is no end to it. There is only the onward surge, people moving towards the town of brick.

As the months went by, Sylvie began to find it unbelievable that there could ever have been a time when she did not know Étienne Roux. The friendship they had formed together, Sylvie realised, was a rare and precious thing; Sylvie felt she knew Étienne as she might a son.

During the champagne break at a concert one afternoon, Étienne told Sylvie about the most important love of his life, the courtship that nearly broke his heart. It happened when he was very young, before his marriage. Sylvie listened closely, watching his lips; her finger traced out the rim of her glass.

Étienne told Sylvie that the woman he so loved he met in Europe. She was the most exquisite creature he had ever seen. She painted; she wore her hair in a velvet snood; she wrote a series of ten poems for him, each a perfect villanelle.

'Ah,' said Sylvie, her voice low because she knew the story would turn out sad. 'What happened to her?'

Étienne shrugged.

'She left,' he said.

'Left? For another, maybe?'

Étienne didn't know. She was an artist, he said. She had other things to do.

'I'm sorry,' said Sylvie.

Étienne shrugged a second time.

'She was exquisite,' he said. 'The most exquisite creature I have ever seen. It was a privilege to love her. It was an experience I will always value. Sylvie, is it a delusion of youth that love then seemed so fine and strong?'

'No,' said Sylvie decisively. 'It's that they don't love like that any more. That is the difference. The world has changed.'

There was pain in her voice; Étienne heard it. He poured her more champagne. He steadied her glass with his hand as he poured.

This, Sylvie then saw in one clear moment, was another experience she must never forget. She must polish it and place it tenderly in her memory. That way it would never disappear.

The second time Annemarie went out in Hoopstad was with Marly from work. Annemarie was grateful to Marly for the invitation; getting out of the flat might help to distract her thoughts.

Marly picked her up at eight.

'Here, I will read out the directions. Remember them,' said Marly when Annemarie had got into the car.

Marly held a piece of torn paper up to the weak car light. The light was reflected in the grease spots on her chin and cheeks. The glitter sprayed on her bare shoulders shone.

'We go all the way down President Street,' Marly read. 'Then, at the Fire Station, left into Market. We follow Market through flatland. Market starts to curve to the right. Then dips. We'll be close to the reservoir. Bugs, it says here, will hit the windscreen.' Marly giggled. 'The guy who gave me these directions is a laugh.' She turned the paper over. 'Now the road will be lined with plane trees. It's not called Market any more but Stone – Stone Street. We continue with Stone – it's still curving to the right. We go through the first roundabout, then, at the second, a big one with aloes in the middle, we go right, and then almost immediately left into Arbuckle Road. Number 129 is right at the end, on the left. It has a smallish front garden and a red door.'

Marly glanced over at Annemarie.

'Got that?' she said.

'Yes,' said Annemarie.

'Then let's go.'

They began to drive down President Street. Annemarie folded her hands over her handbag clasp and gazed out down the bright street ahead of them. It brought an unfamiliar feeling, something almost guilty, being out, especially on a Thursday night. Mother had also thought it a little untoward, but gave her permission after Marly called up. Tonight was Marly's brother's twenty-first birthday party, organised by his university friends.

Marly drew up at a red light.

'Happy?' Marly asked, checking her make-up in the rear-view mirror.

'Yes,' said Annemarie.

They drove on. They came to another red light.

'Is there any chance of Adrian being at the party?' Annemarie asked, still looking straight ahead.

'You mean Adrian van Vuuren?' Marly asked.

'Yes.'

'God, no,' said Marly. 'Adrian at a party? Not a chance.'

They drove on. At the Fire Station they turned left.

'This is Market,' said Annemarie.

'Get off my tail,' Marly said to the car behind them.

Marly looked across at Annemarie.

'You don't crave him or anything, do you?' she asked.

'No,' said Annemarie.

'That's a really good shoe shop. Nice leather stuff. There on our right, just before the flats.' Marly was pointing.

Annemarie leaned forward to look. The street light was in her eyes.

'Good,' said Marly. 'That weirdo turned right at the last intersection. I've heard men like that follow girls home.'

After a while the road began to curve.

'Anyway,' said Marly, 'if I were you I wouldn't get interested in Adrian or anything. He's funny. He doesn't go out or do anything social. You don't know what he does in his spare time. Maybe he hardly ever stops working. He's been out with Sue a bit, but then she's quite strange, too. She's so serious. I don't think I'd feel comfortable with him at all.'

'I was just asking,' said Annemarie.

Annemarie did not remember very much about the party. She knew no one but Marly, who was occupied with her boyfriend, so she stationed herself at the drinks table and tried to look drunk. Before long she actually was drunk: she wasn't much used to cane spirit. Having given Mrs Rudolph her firm promise, Marly drove Annemarie home at eleven.

Even diligent morning paper readers might almost have missed the report, lapping a gap on page eight between the OK advertisement – 'Lightweight, hi-quality, V-necked velour sweaters, colours mauve, camel, teal and black' – and the photograph of the completed foundations – contractor, developers, proud in the foreground – for the new International Hotel. The ceiling of the foyer, says the caption, will be three storeys high. There will be a two-storey-high waterfall fountain. The main front page photograph today in hectic full colour, livening up the news, is of Chef Alfred Brandbuhl at the Victoria and Albert Restaurant in the capital, posing together with a giant blue marlin, which he plans to prepare in such a way and serve to guests on the supper menu. Marlin has never been served on the menu at the Victoria and Albert before – or at any other restaurant in the city, you might imagine. Weather today will be fine, the weather people opine. But everyone knows it's generally sunny our way. No wonder, as it says here, also front page news, that the locus for the battle of Africa moves south. Good old Smithy sticking to Salisbury; the Bishop praying for peace in these troubled times. Sometimes you can't help but worry a little. Like these oil problems. Says that Sunday outings may have to be restricted; so we must read instead the comics, have a *braai*, *boerewors* being on special at Stunt Stores. Well, it can be done, we can econo-mise. There's more to Sundays than Sunday outings, after all: gummy muddle of kids in the back seat, not looking at the oxbow lake, the u-river valley, the fine lines of contour ploughing; not looking but caterwauling. It can be done. There's enough else going on. Look here, for example: American film stars are visiting these parts to open new schools in the Kalahari – though you really might think the blacks already had plenty of such things, and they wreck them as well. Anyway, these stars are coming – also to pick up some of our diamond lustre-clusters on the side, no doubt. Good, in a way, that they do it, shift some positive world interest our way, even if politics as ever dominate the economy. Or at least so says the leader. The minister, on the other hand, says that a satisfactory growth rate is expected for the next financial year. He should know. It's our gold that does it. Which only goes to show, though, that some people, like this editor, have no idea at all. Now look at this Indian couple here, setting out, cheek-to-cheek, cheeky as you please, to dance at the Holiday Inn's Saturday Night Dinner Dance. They have no idea either. The band stopped playing. Mr Greensward, who wrote this letter to the editor, was embarrassed. They were decent people, he says. But they shouldn't have taken the chance and gone out to dance in the first place, should they? It's called stepping out of line. What else is going on? During the past eight years phosphate mines in the lush De Aap Valley have doubled their output. Witch doctors claim to have discovered a cure for cancer of the colon. Good for them – primitive folk brewing something benign for a change. And what's this? It remains unbelievable what these youths get up to. The police have again had to take some action. Well, good for them too. It says that ten prominent young members of the black community were arrested in the township over the weekend. They were asking for trouble yet again. But the second paragraph carries pop-up surprises. One of those arrested was a white man, a doctor even: Dr Adrian van Vuuren (25) of Hoopstad. Police raided his home in the early hours of Saturday morning. Why, you ask yourself, why does a promising young man do it? He could be doing good and useful things with his life. Security police sources have, as yet, refused to say under which act or proclamation these detentions were made. But, the story goes on, it is known that Dr van Vuuren has been involved with community groups based in the townships. These groups have been operating since the time of Steve Biko. Police plan to stamp out their activity. Yes, action like this should certainly do the trick. Sort the guys out. Anything else going on? To Laurie and Laurel a daughter. Thanks to all. In the classifieds an all-purpose milk separator; also, D IY burglar-guarding in a variety of designs – fleur-de-lis, trellis, hound's tooth. What will they think of next? To the end-notes column. What those good old boys in Parliament said last week that was funny. It's sunny and funny our way today. Pity no really good howlers this time, though, to cheer up Monday. Sometimes our fellows make no slips. But she's all right. Sally-Ann Simpson (19) from Khana Bay. No problem there: a good bikini fit. Fold the paper up that way, carefully, so she's looking at you when you open your briefcase. Nothing else like it really, to start the new week.

Étienne usually never telephoned us. If he wanted to contact Mother he would tap at the kitchen window on his way home after work and speak with her through the lattice of coriander and mobile. That early Monday morning, though, when he called us from his office and I answered, hearing his voice laid cool and precise against my ear did not surprise me. In my imaginings such calls were entirely possible. And that Monday, in particular, I was waiting for word. Since Friday, when Adrian had not come to work, I had been hoping for some sort of indication why.

I was expecting a lot. I might have been in love but I knew him hardly at all. He had other friends – other doctors, Sue, perhaps, the men who came to visit him at the clinic. They would be the first to hear if something was wrong. There was, of course, the suitcase. I still had it. When he returned after the three-week absence, he asked me to keep it a little longer. I wondered if that request singled me out? Did it mean he trusted me? He had said, though, that the contents of the suitcase weren't really important – it wasn't much of a favour then. And why should it be? Despite all my hopes, we had not grown much closer. Adrian was so rarely around, and always seemed to be busy. We hadn't talked more than a few times, usually when he gave me rides home. The evening we spent time in his car – after that I had thought my chances with him might improve. The next Friday I could not speak when he came in, I was hoping so hard. But he went on quite as usual. He had walked off to the clinic building with his mail. Each Friday, because of the coming weekend, there was always a great deal of work to get through.

Which is why his absence that Friday was so strange. You couldn't help worrying. I started trying to call Sue; she might have some idea what was wrong. The last few weeks he had been quite reserved and preoccupied. That was maybe why he had avoided staying for a chat. And fewer of his friends had come by. That was also unusual. Then there was also the matter of the suitcase. Perhaps the request to keep it was less an overture of trust, as I wanted to see it, and more an act of expediency. I punched the holes in the telephone dial all the more energetically.

Sue's number did not answer. None of the three van Vuurens in the telephone directory confessed to knowing an Adrian. Adrian had not given me his home number, nor had I ever been home with him. I had no idea where I might find him.

I spent the whole of that weekend in the flat. I wanted to be on hand should news come through. I sat on the floor by the telephone leafing through Mother's magazines. I tried knitting but could not concentrate. Sitting on the floor with the magazines, I mostly stared off into space. From where I was I could only see sky through the window. The unrelieved blueness had no depth.

'What's the matter, my Annemarie?' Mother kept asking. 'You are so strangely quiet. When someone like you, who's quiet anyway, gets quieter, people start to wonder.'

I said I had to contact Sue.

'But what's the urgency?' she asked. 'Is there anything wrong at work?'

I did not reply. I did not want to say more.

Mother was going out with Étienne that night. Towards

the time that he was to call round she grew nervous. Red coronas flared in her cheeks.

'Annemarie, you are not yourself. This makes me uneasy. There's nothing the matter? You know I fret when you're not all right. You can tell me if something's wrong. No more secrets between us. You know that. Just don't make me anxious, is all I ask.'

I said there was a gremlin in the accounts I was doing. I couldn't work it out; perhaps Sue would have advice.

At the sound of Étienne's rapid tapping at the window, we both started. She grabbed my hand.

'Come out to say hello,' she whispered.

The tapping came again, more vigorous, more peremptory.

'Stay up till I return, will you, little one?' She spoke breathily.

I said I would.

But I did not. It was not that I was consciously avoiding Étienne. My suspicions had grown so fantastical they seemed to have separated themselves from the actual man. But I did not much feel like sitting up with him and Mother to talk. Earlier I had fallen asleep on the carpet, next to the telephone. I had strange dreams, the content of which I do not remember, aside from their being full of dread. I awoke in a rank sweat. The carpet beneath me was sodden to the touch. Automatically, without being completely awake, I reached for the telephone. Sue was still not at home. I must have let the phone ring for almost ten minutes. I went to piss and returned. It was still ringing. I went to make tea. When I returned the second time, it had gone dead. I replaced the receiver and went to bed.

But no stillness was to be found there. I got up, unearthed Adrian's suitcase, walked with it around the room, testing its weight. I opened the window, wondered for a moment about throwing it out, then realised that of course Étienne's window faced in the same direction. The thought of its contents, whatever they were, strewn across the quadrangle, made me unexpectedly and intensely nauseous. Another solution might be to take the suitcase out of the flat entirely and stow it somewhere. The bougainvillaea bush at the entrance to the flat building was full and thick enough to provide cover. But then what if I met Mother and Étienne on the stairs or in the lift? I tried dragging the case over to the door anyway, then remembered Mother saying she would put the night-lock on and was taking the key. I went to stack the case back in place, and lay down.

A few minutes later I was up again. Perhaps, I had been thinking, I could get into the case somehow, check the contents. But no, it was securely locked. Even had Adrian's handover been a gesture of trust, it was not a very bold one. Once again I replaced the case, together with the heater, the box, the bear and the other objects of camouflage. Again, I lay down. Soon thereafter, Étienne and Mother returned. They were merry. Mother's laughter skittered around Étienne's low comments. Bottles and ice clunked against glass.

Sue, who had arisen at five-thirty to obtain a morning paper, telephoned the news through to me on Monday morning. She said she had been at home all weekend; she had disconnected the phone. She was hasty.

'I suppose you'd like to know . . . tell the others at work . . . No, no problem at all . . . No, it isn't his first time . . . We'll have to wait and see what happens . . . '

I did not know it was 'not his first time'. I had no idea that he had special experience in these things. Adrian seemed so ordinary, and young, with his acne, his ugly moles. How much had I been missing?

At work no one mentioned him. But then it was not his day for coming in and none of his friends called round. What could also have made a difference was that the clinic that week was again understaffed. No one had time to talk; I spoke only to Marly.

Étienne's call came in the evening.

'Annemarie,' he said – his precise syllable-by-syllable enunciation of my name – 'you're the one I wanted to speak to.'

'Yes?' I replied. And then, at the end of our conversation, once again, 'Yes,' in reply to his courteous goodbye.

'This could just slightly upset your mother,' he said. 'That's why I phoned first. I'll come round to speak to her tonight. It should be all right. The only thing, as I said, is that if you can think of anything to help us, let us know. It would be appreciated. Thank you anyway. I'll see you later.'

'Who was that?' Mother asked as soon as I put down the telephone.

'Étienne.'

'Étienne? For you?'

'He wanted to tell me about Adrian being taken.'

'What? Adrian? That's not your old colleague, is it?'

'Yes, that's right. Adrian van Vuuren. The police have picked him up.' I repeated the words I had just heard spoken. 'Étienne tells me he was detained during the early hours of Friday morning.'

I had maintained my position at the telephone. Next to me was the secretaire. I found I was holding on to the hinge of its winged top. Mother came closer.

'Well, it's nice of Étienne to let you know, I suppose. I wonder if he read it in the papers, or found out at work?'

'He found out at work.'

'That's thoughtful of him.'

'It's part of his job, actually. He wanted to ask if I had

189

anything to tell him – them – the Security Service. You know, anything that might be of use when Adrian's case comes up.'

'What was that you said?' asked Mother. 'You helping the Security Service? Surely not? Surely that can't be?'

I felt Mother's hand fasten on to my own, fixing it to the desk-top hinge.

'Surely it's quite ridiculous,' she said again.

'Not really, Mother,' I said. 'I did work with him. Still, it's not a problem. I know nothing. I have nothing to tell them.'

But Mother was roused; she gripped my hand tighter.

'Then why does Étienne ask you?' she demanded. 'Why? There must be something in it. Please God, Annemarie, if there's something here I don't know, tell me. Let's not go through all this again. The secrecy and silence. Not again. I can't stand it.'

She released my hand, grabbed me at the elbows. The movement brought her too close so she veered off, crying now.

'Mother, I know nothing,' I called after her. 'There's no more I can say.'

The change in Mother, the rapid quickening of her rage and fear was so sudden that I felt helpless. The paranoia of months had been a poor preparation for this. When Mother came round to confront me again, I could not look her in the eye.

'Annemarie,' she now asked, 'how can I possibly believe you? What you say doesn't correspond to what you do. Every-time it's the case. I know that now. And what things don't you do? First with your cousin. Now, for all I know, with this political type. Étienne is astute; he wouldn't ask you about that doctor for no reason. What is it you've been doing? Have you entirely lost your sense of honour? Have you been waiting to deceive me utterly?'

'Mother,' I said, trying to hold her gaze, 'the irony in all this is that I would really have liked to help Adrian with his work. I hoped he might ask me. Perhaps he would have – in time. But the way things stood, he didn't know me well enough. So he didn't. That's the truth.'

Mother brought her head closer to mine. She stood so close I felt her breath moist on my lips.

'You lie,' she said. 'You lie and we both know it. You must know something. I have seen it, you know. I'm not blind. Under your bed – now you can't deny it – there's a suitcase, an old locked one. It's not yours, it's not mine. Whose is it then?' She paused for breath. 'Yes,' she continued more slowly, 'I don't know what's in there but it's heavy. Don't be surprised, I've tested it – I like to know what's going on. So now you try and tell me you know nothing. When I discovered it I was willing to believe it might be something to do with your proper work. But now I see differently. I was foolish to have trusted you. Of course he must be using you. For that and God knows what else. Even in the face of Étienne living next door – in the face of a man of the law who happens also to be my friend.'

I found I could not speak; I had joined her in crying. I sat down on the floor by the telephone, where over the weekend I had waited. She was walking back and forth across the room, shoving at chairs, gingerly picking up objects, looking at them distractedly, putting them down again. She came at me unexpectedly, round the sofa. She was pulling me up by the armpits before she started speaking.

'Get up,' she said. 'Go and fetch that case. Bring it here and open it. If you open it, if the contents are OK, I will believe you. If you won't do it, I insist you take that thing out of this flat and dump it somewhere. I don't want it in my home. But then I'll also know you've been deceiving me again.'

'Mother,' I began to explain, 'I'm not in a position to throw it out. It's not my case.'

'You have it in your keeping. Do it. I am asking you to.'

What could I do? With Mother behind me, I went to the bedroom, crouched down beside the bed, Mother standing over me, removed the heater, the teddy bear, the soup tureen box – all the camouflage objects – then slid out the case.

'Mother,' I said, 'don't make me do this. I only wanted to help. You know how it is. That's why I went to work at the clinic in the first place. I wanted to help. I certainly didn't set out to do wrong.'

'But you did wrong. There's the case and you have no way of explaining it. Like the time before, you had no thought for what your actions could mean. How they would affect me, for example. You have gone against me, your home – against what you have learned to be right. As for me, I may have lost a most valued friend on your account. I think you should try to open that case.'

'I cannot,' I said. 'You know it's locked.'

'Then it must go.'

She pushed me slightly to get me moving. As I was already holding the handle of the suitcase, it banged awkwardly against my legs. She momentarily grabbed my hand again to balance the case.

It was dumped on the flat's rubbish tip. It was so heavy – probably full of pamphlets – we had to swing it up together. It may have stayed there for weeks. From our flat you could not see it. From Étienne's, however, Mother said, you could. The very next day when she was at his place – just spending time trying to get some peace, deciding what to do now, crying a little – she had spotted it. He had called her to the window to see the sunset – a crimson display that ignited the red-brick lengths of Hoopstad. She could see it clearly. She had blushed to stand behind this man whose trust she had, and to be connected with that thing. Étienne had ribbed her. He had asked if the sun had got into her cheeks. But she had not responded. She could have said something, but she had chosen not to. She had wanted to weep out loud. But she had not betrayed me.

'Thank you, Mother,' I said when she told me. 'I'm very grateful to you for that.'

The Rudolphs – mother and daughter – have again left town. Once again, their leave-taking was precipitate and without ceremony. Sylvie Rudolph proposed the move; her daughter Annemarie consented. If they left a forwarding address, Dr Étienne Roux alone would have it. Annemarie did not have an opportunity to bid those at the clinic farewell.

They were out within a few weeks. With time on their hands they packed quickly. As they did once before, they discarded what they could no longer carry with them – the shapes of bad memories – curtains, armchairs and myriad mobiles. This has pleased Dr Roux. Until the new tenants move in, walking past the kitchen window will still remind him of his home and his babyhood.

Dr Roux will miss Sylvie Rudolph. He has enjoyed having a concert companion and charming hostess next door. They got on. That is why he is glad to have done her this good turn – spotting a bit of bad business before it got out of hand. It only goes to show how vigilant one must be, though: even a child from a good nest gets affected. There's no question about it: the negative elements corrupting the country are powerful. The poor Rudolph child had been severely under the influence – wandering about on the factory side of town, holding messages, offering help, wanting to do good deed after good deed. Van Vuuren was only a little slow on the uptake this time. He is a very clever one – difficult to get. What helped was the suitcase Mrs Rudolph told him about: it was full of pamphlets. That was also a good turn she did him. The dear woman had been so worried. Good thing that they could help each other.

In the early evenings, missing the drinks he used to have with Mrs Rudolph, Étienne Roux spends time on his balcony listening to music. The balcony is a feature of corner flats in this building; the Rudolphs were unlucky not to have one. He has his windows slightly open, the speakers facing to outside.

It is almost five o'clock. The record he put on has stopped playing, but still he hums the theme of the final chorus. He beats the heavy bottom of his gin and tonic glass on the balcony rail. Odd how, over at the Rudolphs' flat, the rooms look occupied. It's the fact of the curtains still being up. And those mobiles Mrs Rudolph was silly about. They move about. You might almost believe people were living in there. After all, when they were around, it was sometimes difficult to tell.

Dr Roux turns to face out across Hoopstad. You can't see much because the city is built so low. Today it is also hazy. It must be the fault of the factories. Across the horizon of low roofs lie dark ribbons of cloud. The air is filled with sweetness. The last siren of the day calls. That means time must be getting on. Dr Roux is suddenly aware the music has stopped. His mind runs to supper.